ADVENTURE TIME™

SUGARY SHORTS
VOLUME 2

ADVENTURE TIME: SUGARY SHORTS Volume Two, January 2016. Published by KaBOOM!, a division of Boom Entertainment, Inc. ADVENTURE TIME, CARTOON NETWORK, the logos, and all related characters and elements are trademarks of and © Cartoon Network. (S16) Originally published in single magazine form as ADVENTURE TIME No. 16-18, ADVENTURE TIME 2013 ANNUAL No. 1, ADVENTURE TIME 2013 SUMMER SPECIAL No. 1, ADVENTURE TIME 2013 SPOOOKTACULAR No. 1.

A catalog record of this book is available from OCLC and from the KaBOOM! website, www.kaboom-studios.com, on the Librarians Page.

BOOM! Studios, 5670 Wilshire Boulevard, Suite 450, Los Angeles, CA 90036-5679. Printed in China. First Printing.

ISBN: 978-1-60886-774-5, eISBN: 978-1-61398-445-1

ADVENTURE TIME™
CREATED BY
PENDLETON WARD

"A, YOU'RE ADVENTUROUS"
Written and Illustrated by
ROGER LANGRIDGE

"A SWORD MOST AWESOME"
Written and Illustrated by
ALEX COX

"NO DOGS ALLOWED"
Written by
BRYCE CARLSON
Illustrated by
DUSTIN NGUYEN
Letters by Britt Wilson

"DUNGEONS AND DESSERTS"
Written by
JOSH WILLIAMSON
Illustrated by
JASON HO
Letters by Steve Wands

"THE SUMMITEERS"
Written and Illustrated by
DEREK FRIDOLFS
Colors by Whitney Cogar
Letters by Mad Rupert

"THE LEMON SEA"
Written and Illustrated by
KORY BING & SFE' MONSTER

"DESERT TREASURE"
Written and Illustrated by
NOELLE STEVENSON

"THE SUCKER SEEKER"
Written and Illustrated by
RYAN PEQUIN

"HEART"
Written and Illustrated by
EMILY PARTRIDGE

"A PENNY BURNED"
Written by
FRANK GIBSON
Illustrated by
BECKY DREISTADT

"COSTUME PARTY"
Written and Illustrated by
JONES WIEDLE

"SECRET 'STACHE"
Written by
BRYCE CARLSON
Illustrated by
FRAZER IRVING
Letters by Ed Dukeshire

"HALLOWEEN HORTICULTURE"
Written and Illustrated by
JAY HOLSER

"BAD GIRL GONE GOOD"
Written by
KEVIN CHURCH
Illustrated by
JEN VAUGHN

"OPPOSITE DAY"
Written and Illustrated by
SINA GRACE
Colors by Shaun Steven Struble

"NINJA PRINCESS"
Written by
REED, GRAND & JAI NITZ
Illustrated by
PRANAS NAUJOKAITIS

"SILLY STRING THEORY"
Written and Illustrated by
JAY HOLSER
Colors by Braden Lamb

"PUBLISH OR PERISH"
Written by
RACHEL EDIDIN
Illustrated by
KEL McDONALD

Designer
JILLIAN CRAB

Associate Editor
WHITNEY LEOPARD

Editor
SHANNON WATTERS

With Special Thanks to Marisa Marionakis, Rick Blanco, Nicole Rivera, Conrad Montgomery, Meghan Bradley, Curtis Lelash, Kelly Crews and the wonderful folks at Cartoon Network.

A, YOU'RE ADVENTUROUS

CALGARY COMIC-CON ISSUE TWENTY SEVEN EXCLUSIVE COVER

TAIT HOWARD

A, You're
Adventurous
ROGER
LANGRIDGE

B, you're a
Blunderbuss!

C, I'd Correct you
but I Can't!

D, you're a Dinosaur!
E, you're a big Eyesore!
F, you're a Fanged man-eating plant.

G, it's Gargantuan!
H, you're a Harridan!
I should Invite you to Ignite.
MATCHES
J, just a Jiffy...
K, off a Kliffy...
... and L, I should thank you for the Light.

M...

N...

O...

P...

Maybe Not the Only Plant I see...?

Q... R... S... T!...

Quickly! Run Swiftly up the nearest Tree!

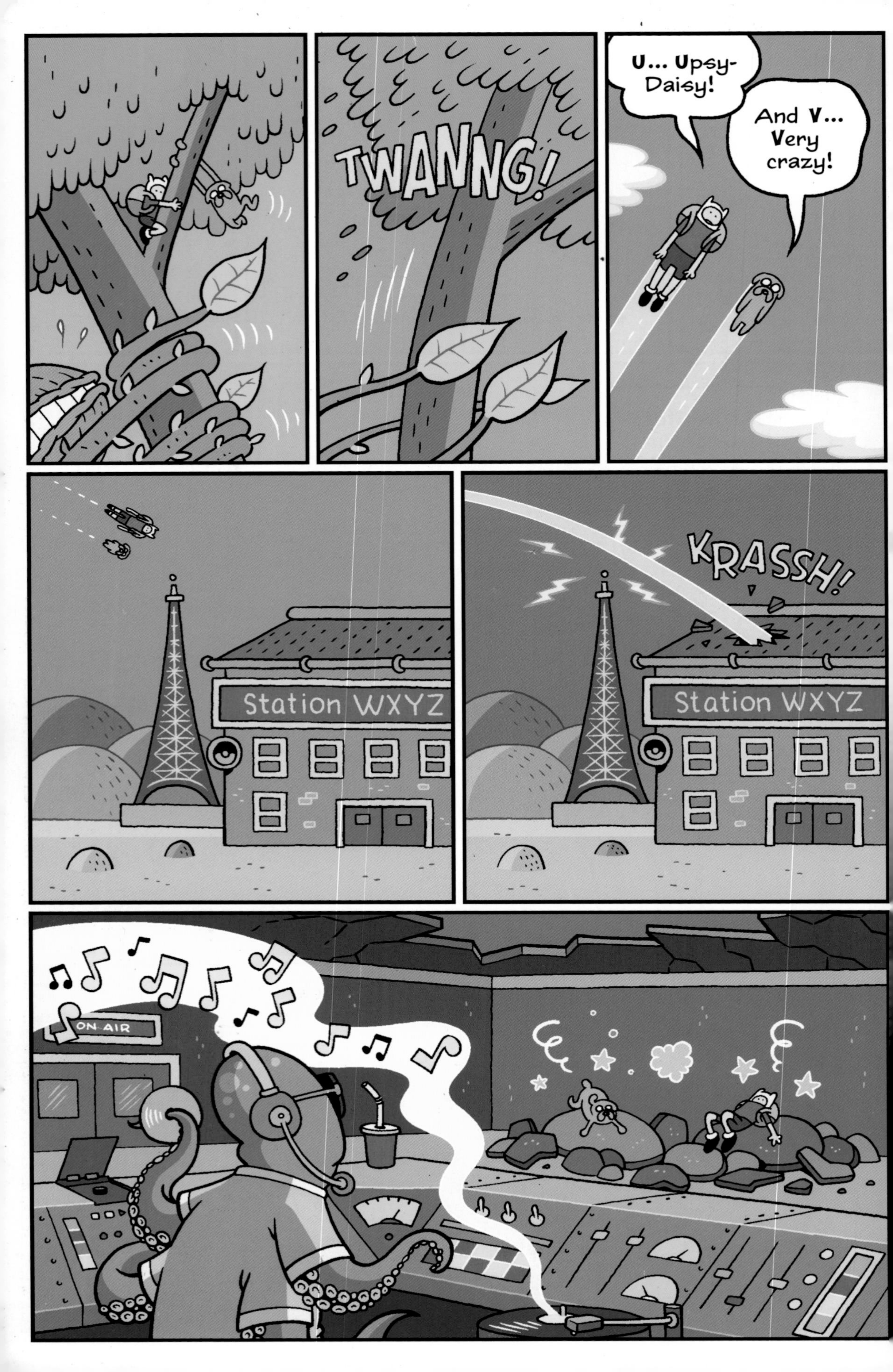
TWANNG!
U... Upsy-Daisy!
And V... Very crazy!
Station WXYZ
KRASSH!
Station WXYZ
ON AIR

FUNGUS and the HERBICIDES
It's fun to wander through the Venus Traps with you!
Forgive me if I disagree.
END.

A SWORD MOST AWESOME

ISSUE TEN, COVER D

NICK EDWARDS

NICK
EDWARDS

a
AN ADVENTURE TIME FINN AND JAKE ADVENTURE! 2013
SWORD MOST AWESOME!
by d.a.cox

This is it... the cave of the GAME-SWORD! If you can win the game, you get a crazy amazing prize!
yo!
ROLL THE DICE!
CLIMB THE ROPE!
START!
JUMP TO BLUE
START OVER :(
LOSE A TURN
FIRE PIT!
OUCH!
JUST CHILL.
GO!
BACK A SPACE
ROLL!
ROLL AGAIN!
AGAIN!
AND AGAIN!
WAIT
OH NO!
FREE PARKING
FIGHT THE BLUE BANGS MONSTER
BLUE!
RED!
SLIDE!
WHEW.
(CHEAT)
HOW'S IT GOING?
GOOD?
OK!
BACK 10 SPACES
BACK 100 SPACES
ARCADE
HIGH SCORE GO!
PEW! PEW!
UP UP
DOWN DOWN
LEFT RIGHT
LEFT RIGHT
B
A
YEAH!
TAKE A BREATH
DON'T CHEAT!
BACK 40 SPACES
BATS!!
WHEEEEEEEE!
BATS?
OH NO!
BATS!
ALMOST THERE....
YOU WIN!
there it is...

woah-ow

IT'S HUGE!

climb climb
pant pant

aw, yeah!!

so shiny

FINN!
YOU DID IT! YOU WON THE GAME!

YOUR PRIZE IS ME, a SWORD MOST AWESOME.
NOW, FINN the HUMAN...
"IMAGINE IT..."
okay.
"WE WOULD BE GIANTS TOGETHER"
"STRONGER THAN A MILLION STRONGS! THE CHAMP!"
"all you have to do..."

...is make ME your best bud! No Jake, or Bubblegum, or Beemo... ME!
ROLL the DICE!
DOMINO!
CHECK-MATE
CHUTE!
DRAW A CARD!
TRIVIA!
LADDER!
DEALER PICKS
CONQUER ASIA!
ROLL AGAIN
SUMP!
GO TO JAIL!
SPIN THE BOTTLE!
KING ME!
BACK 400 SPACES
RACE CAR!
SUMP!
RIGHT FOOT BLUE
GO FISH
BRICK FOR WOOD
ROLL!
what happened? did you win?
that sword was WACK, bro.
ROLL AGAIN!

NO DOGS ALLOWED

ISSUE ELEVEN, COVER C

LOGAN FAERBER

Candy Kingdom Party
NO DOGS ALLOWED
WRITTEN BY BRYCE CARLSON · ART BY DUSTIN NGUYEN · LETTERS BY BRITT WILSON
NO SNIFFING HAMS.
YOU READY TO ROCK THIS PARTY, JIGGETY JAKE?
AHHHH YEAH! LAY DOWN THEM FLOWS, FUNK MASTER FINN.
V-I-P COMIN' ATCHA
LIKE CLEOPATRA
YO DOG, I'LL SCRATCH YA--
WHOA WHOA WHOA
CAN'T YOU READ THE SIGN?
NO DOGS ALLOWED.
HE'S NOT MY DOG...

...HE'S MY FRIEND.
FWOOOOOOSH
AND AN AIRPLANE.
H, SORRY, MISTAKE.
YOU AND YOUR AIRPLANE, ER... I MEAN, FRIEND, CAN COME RIGHT THIS WAY.
V-I-P COMIN' ATCHA
LIKE CLEOPATRA
YO PLANE, I'LL SCRATCH YA--
--NO SNIFFIN' HAMS
BETTER WASH YO' HANDS
CUZ I'M THE MASTA...
I GOT MAD RHYMES
IT'S PARTY TIME
SO GRAB YO' HAMSTA
WORD.

DUNGEONS AND DESSERTS

ISSUE FIFTEEN, COVER C

NIDHN CHANANI

DUNGEONS & DESSERTS
QUEST!
With my massive awesome muscles we have traveled far and wide, my merry Penguins! OH YES!
Finally we are near the magical ICE SWORD that was the focus of this quest!
Isn't that right, Gunter the Green? Tee Hee!
FUN!
Let's get ALL UP in this dungeon!

End Bosses!
Ah jeez, it's FINN THE FEARFUL and JAKE THE DRAGON!
OH, GEOGRAPHY! IT'S THE ICE WARRIOR!
I THINK YOU MEAN, "OH MATH!"
WHATEVER, JAKE THE DRAGON! WHY ARE YOU SO MEAN ALL THE TIME?!
SO MEAN!
BRING IT ON, ICE WARRIOR!
Attack Formation!!!
IT IS BROUGHT'EN!

Skirmish!
VICTORY!
UNCLE! UNCLE!
HAHAHA TEE HEE TEE HEE!
That's right! I am the winner! The Ice Sword in the Ice Cream will be...
Champion!
WHHAAAAAA?? "CHAMPION?!"
Gunter the Green?! I thought you were my FRIEND?!

No, No, NO!
I'm the Dessert Master I should be the one to win the Ice Sword.
It's in my name!
ICE KING!
ICE SWORD! ICE?!
DUNGEON & DESSERTS

I'm never playing with you again, Gunter. You cheat!
DUNGEONS & DESSERTS
WINK!
END.

THE SUMMITEERS

ISSUE TWENTY FOUR, COVER C

KEVIN STANTON

맛있어 보여요
AW SHUCKS! IT'S A RENTAL.
AND NO WAY THESE GUYS ARE STOPPING ME FROM GETTING MY DEPOSIT BACK.

GET BEHIND ME, LADY RAINICORN.
IT'S TIME TO MAKE SOME MUSIC—
WAKE UP, SLEEPY HEAD...

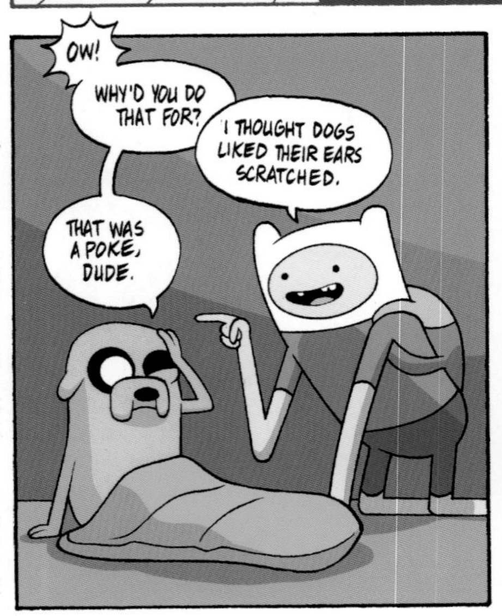
OW!
WHY'D YOU DO THAT FOR?
I THOUGHT DOGS LIKED THEIR EARS SCRATCHED.
THAT WAS A POKE, DUDE.

I HEAR WITH THOSE, YOU KNOW.
QUIT BEING SO SENSITIVE.
YOU QUIT BEING AN EAR WAX THIEF!
TODAY'S THE DAY!

DOES IT INVOLVE SLAYING OGRES?
I DON'T THINK SO.
THEN REMIND ME AGAIN WHAT WE'RE DOING?
WE'RE CLIMBING THE TALLEST MOUNTAIN IN OOO!

NOT THAT ONE.
I'M NOT THE TALLEST?
NO WAY. BUT YOU ARE THE NICEST.
THANK YOU.

NOT YOURS EITHER, ICE KING!
CURSE YOU, FINN, WITH MY SHAKING COLD FIST OF DOOM.

I'M GUESSING THAT ONE.
GOOD GUESS, JAKE!
IT'S WHAT I DO.

NUTS, THE SKY LOOKS ALL WEEPY.

YOU SURE YOU WANNA MAKE THE HIKE WEARING THAT?

WHY NOT? I'M ALWAYS DRESSED FOR ADVENTURE!
A LITTLE RAIN CAN'T STOP ME.

SPLOOSH

YOU'RE RIGHT. LET'S GO, WATER-BUDDY!

ARE... WE... THERE...
...YET.....

UM, WE HAVEN'T EVEN LEFT BASE CAMP...
AWWWWWWW..
MUST BE THE HIGH ALTITUDE.
THE LACK OF OXYGEN IS MAKING YOUR BRAIN-JELLO ALL SNOOZY.

FINE... JUST... GO... ON WITHOUT... ME... I... CAN'T... ...TAKE... ANOTHER... ...STEP...
OR A FIRST STEP...
SHUT... ...UP....

WHY WALK WHEN YOU CAN BE CARRIED?
WHAT THE FISH?!
WHO SAID THAT?

I DID.

NOPE, I WAS RIGHT THE FIRST TIME.
THAT ENCHANTED RAINCLOUD MADE YOUR BACKPACK ALL SENTIENT.
WHAT DO YOU DESIRE, OH MAGIC SACK?

TO RETURN THE FAVOR.
SINCE YOU ALWAYS CARRY ME,
I SHALL NOW CARRY YOU.
UM... I GUESS THAT'S COOL.

THIS... IS... MATHEMATICAL!
I WISH I HAD MY BACKPACK.

WHAT ARE YOU SUPPOSED TO BE?
Chuckle Chuckle
YOU SURE ARE DUMB, I'M A WALKING STICK FOR OUR HIKE, SILLY.
MAYBE YOU CAN FIND ONE PACKED INSIDE YOUR MOUTH.

WHAT WAS THAT?
BBLOORSH
HE JUST SPIT UP EVERYTHING YOU PACKED.
HE'S LIKE A GIANT FABRIC SLOT MACHINE.
YUP, HERE'S YOUR WALKING STICK.

HEY, CAN YOU HEAR THAT?
MY NOW EMPTY WAXLESS EARS ARE PICKING UP SOMETHING NEARBY.

CLANG!
KLUNGG!
CLANGG!

I THINK YOU STOLE MY EYE WAX TOO!
SKI NINJAS **AND** SURF SAMURAIS...
FIGHTING ONE ANOTHER...
OUTSIDE THEIR NATURAL HABITATS?!
THIS IS DONKERS!

WHAT THE BATTICLE?!
I CAN'T SEE ANYTHING FROM BACK HERE!
MY HANDS ARE FUSED!
WOW! YOU JUST MISSED A ONCE IN A LIFETIME EVENT!

BUT HEY, YOU'VE GOT MORE THAN ONE LIFE, RIGHT CHUM?
I DON'T THINK SO.
BEING HUMAN SUCKS.

WHOA! HOLD UP!
YOU SEE WHAT I SEE?

WHO ARE THEY?
YETI CONGRESSMEN, DEBATING SNOW POLITICS.
giggle!
AND THEY'RE IN LITTLE SUITS...TEE HEE!

I CALL THIS MEETING TO ORDER!
NO I CALL THIS MEETING TO ORDER!

WELL THEN, I ORDER THIS MEETING TO CALL!
WHAT DID YOU CALL ME?!
QUIT FILIBUSTERING!
DON'T MAKE ME BUST YOU, PHIL!

PLEEEEEEZE... JUST TURN AROUND.
I CAN'T... SEE ANYTHING!

MAN, POLITICS IS SO BORING.
LET'S GO.

HEY BACK-PACK!
RACE YA TO THE TOP!

THE GROUND. WHY DOES IT SHAKE?
RUMBLE
RUMBLE
ONLY CUZ IT'S SCARED OF HOW RADICAL WE ARE.
OR MAYBE IT'S TICKLISH.

SNIIIFFFF
MY NOSE-O-SCOPE IS PICKING UP SOMETHING APPROACHING FAST!

FINN, ARE YOU ALLERGIC TO DAIRY?
I DON'T THINK SO.
RRUMBLLE
HOW 'BOUT SNOW?

MOUNTAIN GOAT CHEESE RACE

SNIFF
SNIFF
DON'T WORRY, BOY. I'LL DIG YA OUT.

COFF

WHAT TOOK YOU SO LONG?
MMPH... I CAN'T DIG ON AN EMPTY STOMACH...MMPHH.

WE DID IT!
WE REACHED THE TOP!
eerp–
WHEW, I'M BUSHED.
AND A LITTLE GASSY FROM THE CHEESE...

YAY FOR YOU. YOU DIDN'T MISS EVERYTHING FACING THE OTHER DIRECTION.

CHEER UP, DUDE. YOU HARDLY MISSED MUCH.
JUST THE MOST AWESOME DAY EVER!!!

SUMMITEERS!!
BUMP

THAPP

WHY'D YOU GO AND DO THAT FOR?!
NOW WE'LL NEVER HAVE MORE ADVENTURES WITH HIM!
HE DESERVED IT. THAT WAS MY STICK-OF-FORGETFULNESS.
WHICH GIVES ME AN IDEA...

HMMM...
SOOOO, THIS IS KINDA WEIRD, DON'T YOU THINK?
더많은 차 바랍니다
OF COURSE, MY SWEET.

HEY! YOUR FINGER WAS IN MY—
I'M NOT AFTER YOUR EAR WAX.
WE'RE GONNA CLIMB THE TALLEST MOUNTAIN AGAIN.
AGAIN?
ERR...I MEAN, FOR THE FIRST TIME, YEAH!

YOUR BACK'S NAKED. AREN'T YOU FORGETTING SOMETHING?
NOPE, I'VE GOT EVERY-THING I NEED.

SPLOOSH

WHOA!
NICE DODGE!
THAT ANGRY CLOUD SPIT AT YOU!
HAH!
BARELY FELT A DROP!

UMM...
DUDE...
YOUR HAT IS EATING YOUR FACE.

ARGGHHHHH!!
HE SHOULD'VE JUST WORE HIS BACKPACK.

END.

THE LEMON SEA

2013 SUMMER SPECIAL, COVER C
ROB GUILLORY

The Lemonsea
by Sfé Monster & Kory Bing
Beach Access
Any Unauthorized or Unacceptable activities will result in
Twelve years Dungeon
NO TRIAL.
by order of the
Earls of Lemongrab

LOOK. THE LEMON SEALS HAD A LEMONLING.
WE WILL CALL YOU NUBBINS.
COME. LET US SET UP FOR THE PICNIC.
MWEH.

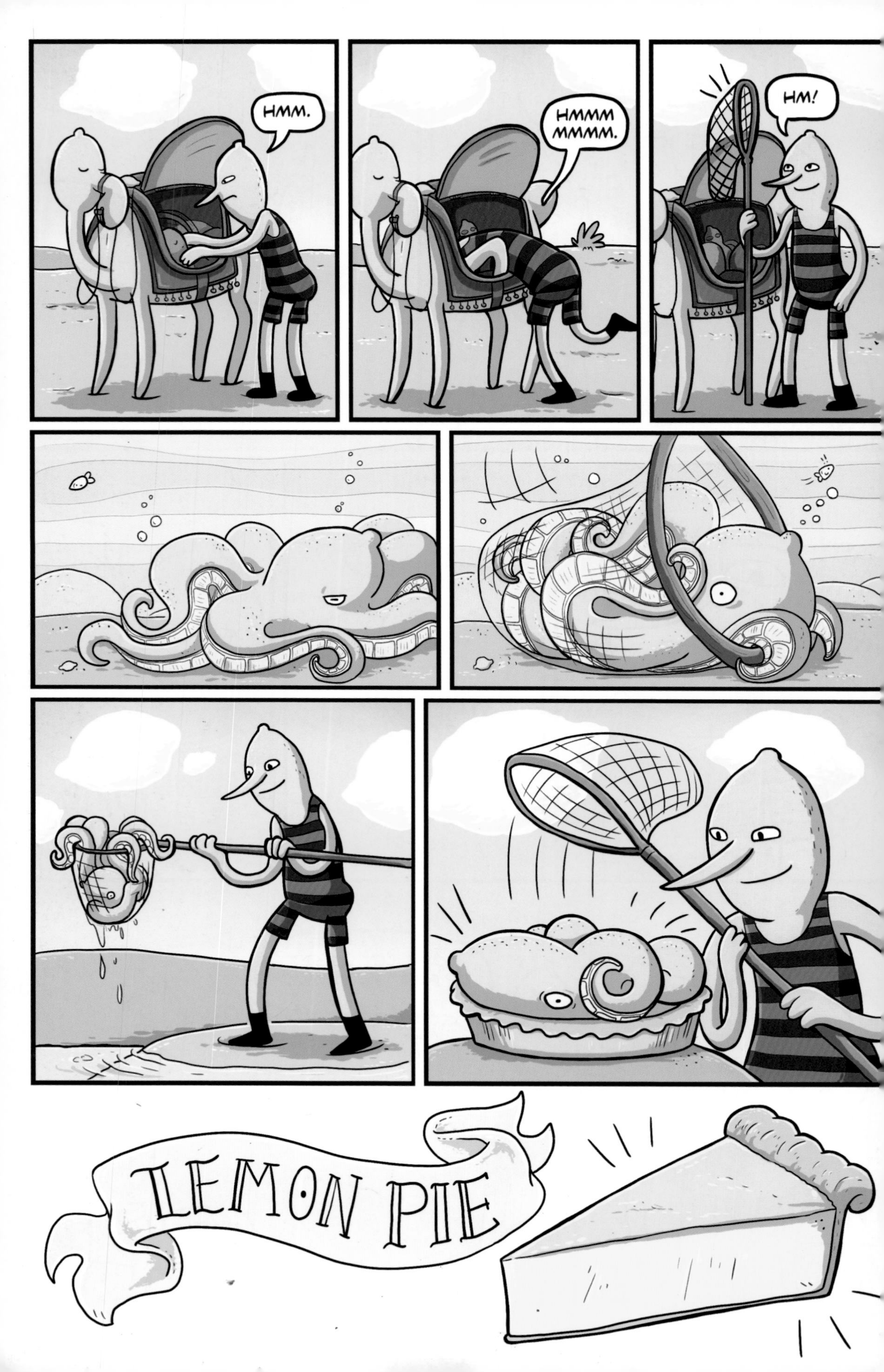
HMM.
HMMM MMMM.
HM!
LEMON PIE

Lemon Jelly
LEMON JELLY ON BREAD!

HMMMMMMMMMMMM
MMMMMMMMMMMM
MMMMMMMMMMMM
SPLASH
SQUEEZE
Fresh-Squeezed Lemonade!

Acceptable.
HEY!!
???
WHAT ARE YOU TWO DOING TO THESE POOR DEFENSELESS LEMON CREATURES!?
WE ARE HAVING A PICNIC.
HMMM. WOULD YOU LIKE TO JOIN US?
OH! HEY, IS THAT LEMONADE?
THE END!

DESERT TREASURE

ISSUE TWENTY SEVEN, COVER B
JJ HARRISON

DESERT TREASURE
Man, we're lost! I told you you're reading that thing upside-down!
by Noelle Stevenson
No we're not! see, there's Butt Butte!
The secret Tunnel should be right over that-a-ways!

Well, what are we waiting for?

KAPWINGG

AAAAHH
WHUMP

AAAAHH
FLOP

Greetings, Troll Guardian Guy!
We seek the Desert Treasure. Is this the secret Tunnel?

I can't tell you! It's a secret!

Um... the SIGN says it's the secret Tunnel...
SECRET TUNNEL

Okay fine it is the secret Tunnel. But you cannot pass without paying the toll!

Aw dang! The map didn't say this was a toll road.
That will be five gold.

But we're broke as all get-out!
Then no tunnel for you!

How's a kid supposed to make a quick buck in the middle of the desert anyway?
Dude, I've got it!
We'll have a lemonade stand for thirsty travelers!
Yeah! Awesome!
But – we don't have any lemons.
Psh, details.
We can just use these cactus blossoms!
I forget, are these poisonous?
Eh, they're probably fine.
If we add enough sugar, no one will even notice!
Good thing I never leave home without massive quantities of sugar.
SUGAR

LEMONADE
$ BUY IT! $
Oooh lemonade! Aren't you just the cutest!

GLUG
GLUG
GLUG

PSSSHH

This stuff is rank and warm! Give me my money back!

Aw man, I knew we should've packed ice cubes!
It's okay dude, there will be more travelers!

PSSSH

PSSHH

PSSH
PSSSH

PSSH
PSSH
PSSH

YOO HOO!
Oh great! Look who's coming NOW.

No one likes our lemonade! How are we gonna get cash for the secret Tunnel now?

Oh boy, Lemonade! I DID forget to pack a refreshing beverage to keep my insides cool while my outsides get all bronzed and sexy!

No way, Ice King! We're not selling you any lemonade!
Yeah, move it along! You'll scare our customers!

Gah! FINE! If I can't have any...

...NOBODY can have any! YAHHH!
ZAP!
LEMONAD

Geez! Ice king turned our lemonade into solid chunks!

Whoa hey! Are those ice pops? I could super go for one of those!

Mmnnghh mmmm
Dang, that hits the spot! I'll take your whole stock, dudes!

Aw yeah, HECKA cash!
we could go through that tunnel like twenty times now!
LEMONAD

Who even needs that treasure now!
We're rich! Woohoo!
THE END

THE SUCKER SEEKER

ISSUE TWENTY THREE, COVER B
SEO KIM

seo KIM

RYAN PEQUIN

THE SUCKER SEEKER

♪ PUTTIN' PEPPER ON MY EGGS ♫

♪ THIS IS A SONG... ABOUT EGGS! I— ♫

COO

AHH!

OH. HEY FINN.

UH, WHY IS THERE A BIRD?

I RESCUED HIM.

HE WAS STUCK IN MY UNDERWEAR DRAWER.

HA, WEIRD. WHY ARE YOU HOLDING HIM WITH TONGS?
I READ SOMEWHERE THAT BIRDS ARE HECKA FULL OF DISEASES
OH. GOOD CALL THEN. YOU GONNA SHOO HIM OUTSIDE OR WHAT'S THE PLAN?
I TRIED! HE WOULDN'T GO FOR SOME REASON
I WAS THINKING MAYBE HE COULD STAY HERE FOR A LITTLE WHILE.
I DUNNO, MAN. I'M NOT SUPER INTO THE IDEA OF KEEPIN' PETS.
NAH, DUDE! IT WOULDN'T BE LIKE THAT! HE'D BE, LIKE, A ROOMMATE!
HE CAN JUST HANG FOR A COUPLE DAYS, CHECK OUT OUR "VIBE."
WELL WE DO HAVE A PRETTY SWEET VIBE. AND HE'S PRETTY ADORABLE FOR A BAG FULL OF GERMS AND MITES.
HEH HEH I'M JUST MESSIN' WITH YOU, MAN.

TWO WEEKS LATER:
FINN! HAVE YOU SEEN MY TEAPOT?
NO! HAVE YOU SEEN MY PANTS ??
I LOST MY ONLY PAIR. NOW I GOTTA KICK IT IN MY SKIVS!
WHY'S ALL OUR STUFF GOIN' MISSING?
SOMEONE KEEPS EATING MY HOME-MADE CALZONES TOO! I LEFT A NOTE BUT THEY JUST TOOK IT OFF. VERY RUDE!
BMO'S C-ZONE DO NOT EAT!
BMO
TOOOOOOT
WHAT'S THAT?
MY TEAPOT!
AW, GROSS! BIRD!! I NEVER SAID YOU COULD USE MY STUFF AS A HOT TUB!
AND THERE ARE MY SHORTS! DON'T USE MY SHORTS TO DRY OFF! HEY!!
YOU'RE GETTIN' BIRD GUNK ALL OVER MY DUDS, DUDE!
YOU'RE BEING A MAJOR BUTT, BIRD.

THE BIRD DIDN'T DO THE DISHES EITHER AND IT'S HIS TURN!
BIRD, YOU'RE ... A CRUDDY ROOMMATE.
I HATE TO SAY THIS, BUT I THINK IT'S TIME FOR YOU TO LEAVE.
YEAH. YOU GOTTA GO BACK TO YOUR NEST OR WHATEVER, DUDE.
NO...
OH! YOU CAN TALK...?
THAT'S ... NOT...
WHOA

FAIR!!

SWAT
OOF!
WHAT THE HECK IS GOING ON?!
IT'S A SUCKER SEEKER!
BOOM
THEY SEEK OUT PEOPLE THEY THINK ARE "SUCKERS" AND LEECH OFF OF THEM!
THEY WEASEL THEIR WAY INTO PEOPLES' HOMES, EAT THEIR FOOD, AND HAVE LOUD PARTIES WITHOUT CLEANING UP AFTER!
YOU MONSTER!
WOOSH
YAAAAAH!
LEAP

BREAK
WHOA! HIS STEEZ WAS TOO MUCH FOR MY SWORD!
ATTACKS ONLY MAKE HIM STRONGER!
HIS ONLY WEAKNESS IS—
NUHH!!
CHOMP!
DEMOCRACY!!
PLRP!
HUH?
A VOTE!
BMO
WE HAVE TO PUT IT TO A HOUSE VOTE!!
BMO

I DON'T GET IT
TRUST ME!
UH, OK! HOUSE VOTE! WHO WANTS THE GROSS LEECH MONSTER TO MOVE OUT?
ME.
ME!
PLRP!
MMF!
AAGH!! HOW DID YOU KNOW?!
PTOO!
GUH
THUD
JUST WHEN YOU THINK YOU FOUND A REAL SUCKER TO TAKE ADVANTAGE OF...
DUDE! HOW?
THE LEECH CODE SAYS THEY HAVE TO OBEY HOUSE VOTES!
I'VE HAD A BUNCH OF ROOM-MATES AND LIKE NINETY PERCENT OF THEM WERE LEECHES IN DISGUISE.
ALSO, UH
THINK YOU COULD PUT YOUR PANTS BACK ON? THE SKIVVIES ARE WEIRDIN' ME OUT A BIT.
THE END

HEART

ISSUE TWENTY TWO, COVER B
ALLEN LAU

HEART
BY EMILY PARTRIDGE
MODIFIED CANDY GOLEM
G IN THERE

OOO
MAP

"CRYSTAL HEART"
NATURALLY OCCURING POWER SOURCE
(UNTESTED)
TEST ON CANDY GOLEM
– BENEFITS VS. SCIENTIFICALLY ENGINEERED 'HEART'?

UNIDENTIFIED MATERIAL—
CAMP AND GATHER SUPPLIES IN A.M.
* BLOWTORCH?

END

A PENNY BURNED

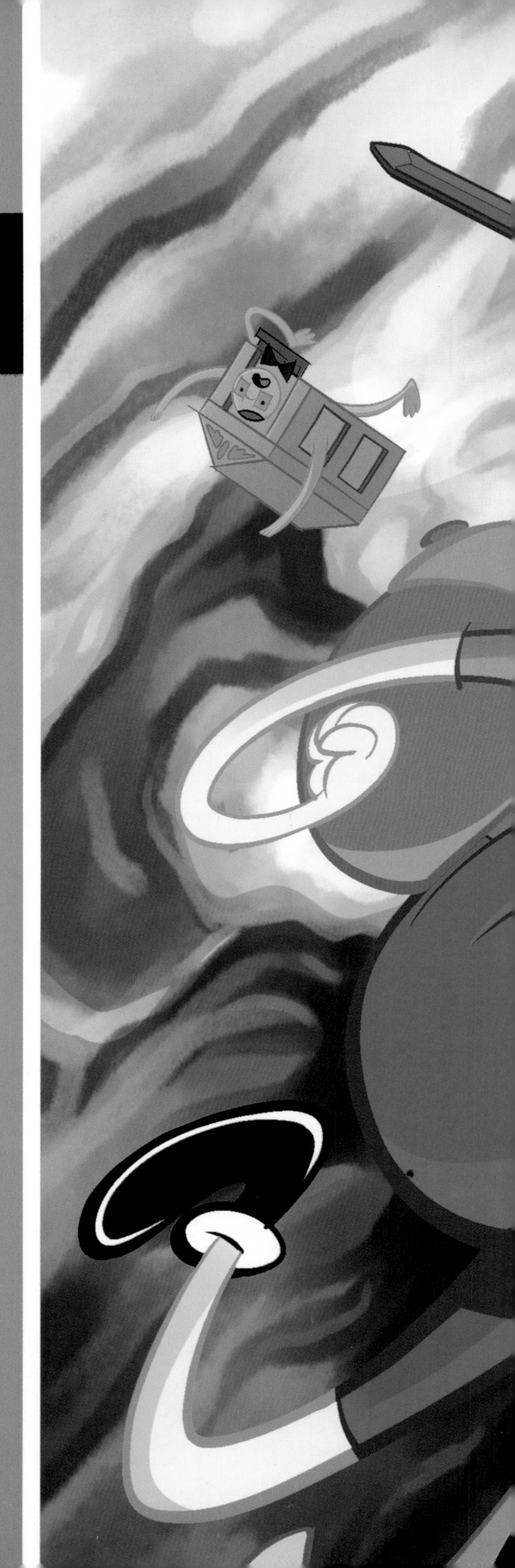

ISSUE FIFTEEN, COVER D
SPIKE TRAUTMAN

Fionna and Cake in
A PENNY BURNED!
This yard, y'know, it's just so dirty. I hate a dirty yard, don't you?
I can clean this up in no time at all, Mr. Stumps!

Take a gander!

Hee
Hee

Yes ma'am this is one clean yard.

Here's a little something extra for your hardship, ladies.

Yes! We've finally saved enough to attend the Heroes & Adventurers Caucus!

Plus two dollars.
Yeah! If we head over there now I can get in line and maybe get a limited edition statuette or something.
Gosh darn these leaves.

That money is already burning a hole in your pocket.

No it isn't! I'm just-
YOU GOTTA GET RID OF IT!

AHAAAAAH!

AHHAAHHHhhhhhh

Take it! Take it all!
TICKETS

TICKETS

NO SHIRT,
NO SHOES,
NO GIRLS.

Take it easy, sweetheart. The caucus is a place where us heroes can feel safe in displaying masculinity. You know, without the judgemental eyes of *women*.

TICKETS

TICKETS

I can't even go? This is bogus!
They aren't worth it, pumpkin.

I'm going.

How are we going to get in?

This doesn't seem very heroic, Fionna.

I guess not.
BOY

CRASH

My apologies, fellow hero!
BOY

Haha! No way I'm a hero! I'm just dressed up as my favorite one. Who are you dressed up as?

Just some idiot.
Cool! I love barbarians! I' show you my favorit one
BOY

Gavlar the Bewhiskered! He once rode the carcasses of a hundred slain beasts into the center of a volcano!

He looks so sad.

SMOOCH

That guy is sure doing a lot of foot kissing.
Why are you kissing feet, little guy?
I need to do this, I need to keep them happy!

This is their reward for a life well-lived! They were once great men.

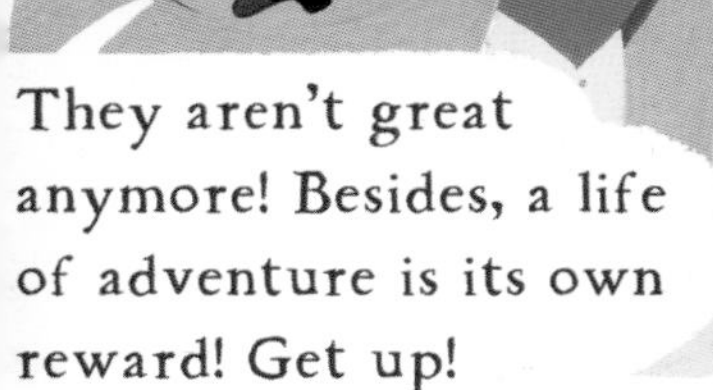
They aren't great anymore! Besides, a life of adventure is its own reward! Get up!

You, child! Get back to kissing or I will kick you into subserviency!

Not before I kick you into space!

ARGH!!

What is your name, brave knight?

Fionna!
And I'm Cake! A girl cat!

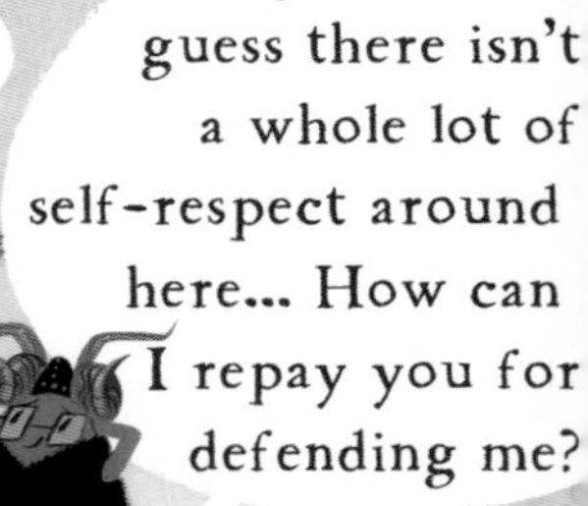
That's right! We're women and better than everybody!
Oh, hey guys! I'm sorry I was doing all that, I guess there isn't a whole lot of self-respect around here... How can I repay you for defending me?

A couple of bucks would be nice.
What?

HA HA HA!

No but seriously this costume cost way more than it should have and I'm broke.

COSTUME PARTY

ISSUE EIGHTEEN, COVER B
KELLY BASTOW

Costume Party!
HMMM...
HMMMMM...
FINN + JAKE ARE HAVING A PARTY AND I WASN'T INVITED?
WHAT THE HECK!

WHY WOULDN'T YOU INVITE THIS TO A PARTY?
EH? EH? YOU KNOW WHAT I'M SAYIN', GUNTER?
WENK.
YOU NEVER KNOW WHAT I'M SAYIN', GUNTER.
I'LL SHOW FINN AND JAKE JUST WHAT THEY'RE MISSING OUT ON...
I'LL SHOW THEM......
'SUP.
GASP!!!

OH MY GLOB. YOUR ICE KING COSTUME IS. SO. LEGIT!
SAY WHA?
WOW, LIKE, I REALLY DIG THE BEARD!
HUH?
YOU'VE REALLY CAPTURED HIS 'REPULSIVE' AURA!
HE EVEN SMELLS LIKE CABBAGE, JUST LIKE THE REAL THING!
HEY!
SO REALISTIC!
DANCE WITH US!
DANCE WITH US!

WHOEVER THAT IS, THEY'RE KILLIN' IT!
oo0Ooo!
TWIRL
AAAAA!
YEAH, BUT WILL THEY BE KILLIN' IT AT THE COSTUME CONTEST?
HA HA! WHAT DO YOU THINK, MARCELINE?
HMM... WE'LL SEE.

LISTEN UP! IT'S COSTUME JUDGING TIME!
LET'S SEE WHICH OF YOU LIVES UP TO THE VAMPIRE QUEEN'S STANDARDS!
WHY DON'T WE START WITH YOU?
EH?
YAAAAY!
HUH???
ALL RIGHT! LET'S SEE THE GENIUS BEHIND COSTUME #1!
O-OW! HEY!!
HEY! THAT'S NO ICE KING COSTUME! THAT'S THE REAL THING!
NOBODY CRASHES MY PARTY AND GETS AWAY WITH IT! ESPECIALLY NOT ICE KING!

KNOCK IT OFF, BOZO!
MARCELINE, WHAT THE HECK! HE'S GOING TO TRY AND KIDNAP PRINCESSES!
SIMON, WHY ARE YOU HERE?
I SAW THAT FINN + JAKE WERE THROWING A PARTY. IT LOOKED LIKE FUN... I WANTED TO JOIN TOO.
SEE? HE'S HARMLESS.
.......FFFFINE. I GUESS YOU CAN STAY, ICE KING.
WOO!
YOU DID THE RIGHT THING, DORK.
I GUESS EVEN EVIL DUDES DESERVE TO HAVE A LITTLE FUN ONCE IN AWHILE.
HECK YEAH! BUT ONLY WHEN THEY'RE NOT BEING EVIL.
HA HA! YEAH.
END.
J.N. WIEDLE

SECRET 'STACHE

2013 SPOOOKTACKULAR SPECIAL, COVER B
MING DOYLE

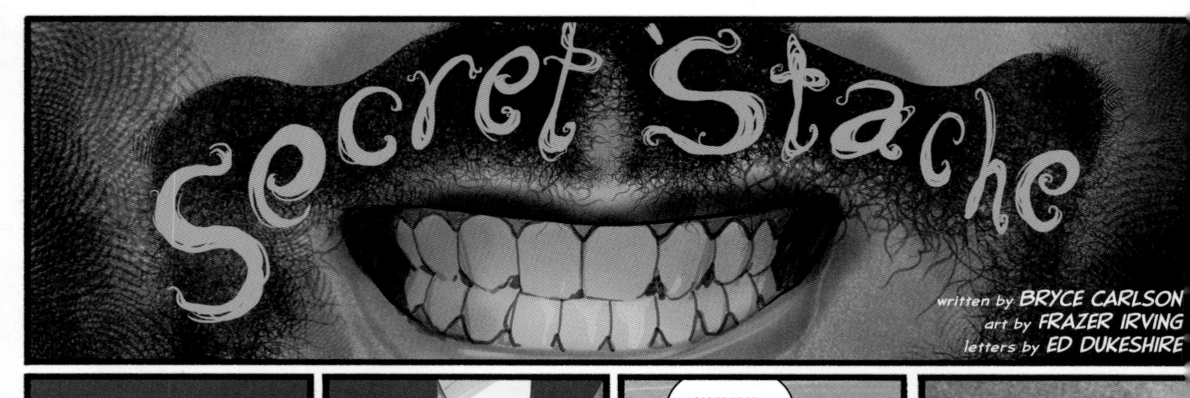
Secret 'Stache
written by BRYCE CARLSON
art by FRAZER IRVING
letters by ED DUKESHIRE

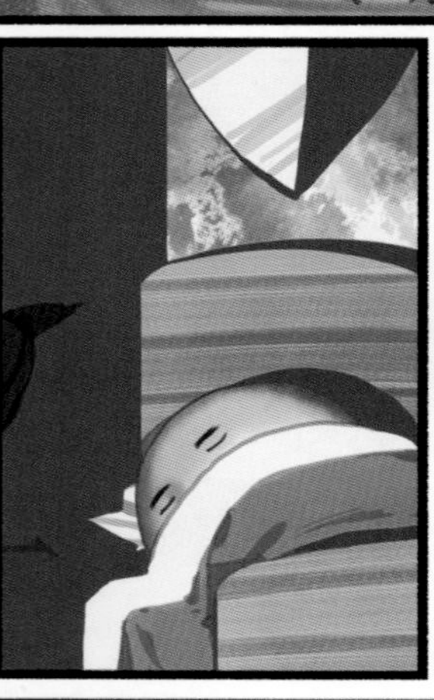

HMMMM...

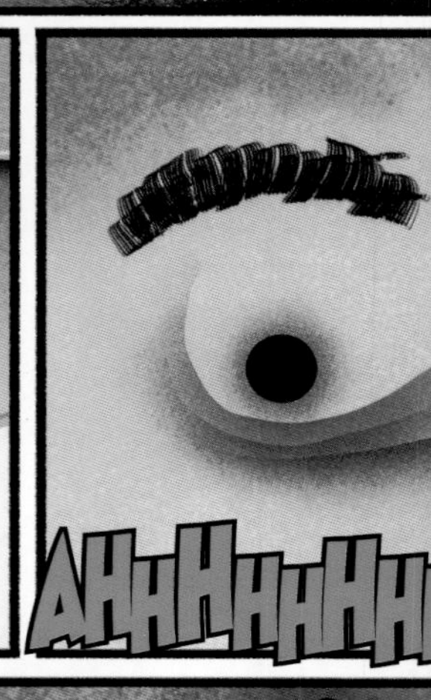
AHHHHHHH

WHERE ARE YOU? COME ON NOW...DON'T SCARE ME LIKE THIS!
WE NEVER GOT TO GO FISHING TOGETHER LIKE I ALWAYS PROMISED... HOW WE SUPPOSED TO FISH IF--

STARCHY LOST HIS MUSTACHE!

FINN! JAKE! IT'S ME, STARCHY THE GRAVEDIGGER, AND I'M IN A WHOLE HEAP OF TROUBLE!
GOT A MUSTACHE GONE ROGUE--!
WHOA, TAKE IT EASY THERE, MAN-CHEGO. WE KNOW STARCHY. HE HAS A TOTALLY SWEETLES MUSTACHE. WHERE'S YOUR 'STACHE, BRO?
CAREFUL, FINN, THIS GUY LOOKS LIKE A REAL WEIRDO, LIKE HE'S ALL GLOBBED UP, DON'T KNOW WHAT TO DO AND STUFF.
WAIT, WHERE YOU GOING, LITTLE DUDE? WE CAN'T HIP-HOP-HELP IF YOU RUN AWAY.
LET HIM GO, FINN. IT'S TEA TIME.
AHHHHHHHH!
PRINCESS, I TOLD YOU, IT'S ME... STARCHY THE GRAVEDIGGER!
FEAR NOT, CONFUSED LITTLE DOUGH MAN, PEP BUT AND I KNOW SOMEONES WHO CAN TELL US WHO YOU REALLY ARE AND HELP FIND THIS MOO-STASH YOU KEEP RAMBLING ABOUT.
HUH-BUH... HUH-BUUUUH... H-H-H...

I DON'T SEE ANYTHING, STRANGER. IT'S LIKE YOU DON'T EXIST.
WHAT DO YOU SEE, BROTHER?
CAAAWWWW!

FEAR FART

LOOK, IT'S STARCHY!
STARCHY'S HERE EVERYBODY!
WHERE YOU BEEN, STARCH-MEISTER?

WOOOOOOOOOSH
WAIT, THIS GUY DOESN'T EVEN HAVE A MUSTACHE!
IMPOSTER! GET HIM!

COME HERE, YOU LITTLE NAKED FACE FREAK!
YOUR SMOOTH UPPER LIP IS OFFENSIVE TO ME!
NO, PLEASE, DON'T HURT OL' STARCHY! I'M JUST TRYING TO FIND MY MUSTACHE SO WE CAN GO FISHING TOGETHER LIKE I ALWAYS PROMISED!

YOU AIN'T GOIN' ANYWHERE...WE'RE GONNA 'STACHE YOU, BOY. GONNA 'STACHE YOU NICE AND GOOD.
TASTE MY WHISKERS!

SWIFF
SWIFF
SWIFFERY
SWIFF
ULP, STARCHY'S GONNA THROW UP...

MAKE IT STOP! I DON'T EVEN WANT A MUSTACHE ANYMO--

OOF... OUCH... OOCH...

THERE YOU ARE...YOU LOOK GLORIOUS... STARCHY WAS SO SCARED--

QUIET NOW, FELLA, YOU'LL SCARE MUSTACHE'S FISH AWAY.

HALLOWEEN HORTICULTURE

2013 SPOOOKTACKULAR SPECIAL, COVER A
BECKY DREISTADT

HALLOWEEN HORTICULTURE
by JAY HOSLER
ARE YOU SURE TREE TRUNKS SAID THIS WOULD BE A SHORTCUT TO HER HOUSE?
I **THINK** SO.
SHE DEFINITELY SAID **SOMETHING.**
I WASN'T REALLY LISTENING.
WE CAN'T BE LATE, MAN.
WE'LL GET THERE.
AND THIS WAY HAS MORE THORNS AND STUFF TO SCRATCH US UP.
WE DO LOOK PRETTY RUGGED.
SEE?
UPSIDE!
HA, HA. YEAH.
BOOo HOOo HOOoo
WHOA, DUDE, THAT PRINCESS LOOKS **BUMMED**.
ON HALLOWEEN NIGHT?
BUT THIS IS THE HAPPIEST TIME OF THE YEAR, BABY.
HEY, HEY, HEY, GIRL. LET US SOOTHE YOUR GENTLE BROW.
sniff
...it's too... late...
i... i need a hero b-before midnight...

WILL TWO RIGHTEOUS HEROES DO?
BELIEVE IT, PRINCESS!
REALLY?

WOULD WIMPY DUDES BE ALL COVERED IN SCRATCHES AND BLOOD AND SUCH?
OH, THIS IS WONDERFUL!
YEAH, WE GET THAT A LOT.

I AM PUMPKIN PRINCESS AND I CARRY A TERRIBLE BURDEN.
SOMEWHERE INSIDE MY HEAD, IS A BAD SEED.
IF IT ISN'T DESTROYED BEFORE MIDNIGHT ON HALLOWEEN, I WILL TURN INTO A RAMPAGING, CANDY EATING BEAST AND CONSUME THE CANDY KINGDOM!

THAT IS NOT GONNA HAPPEN!
HOW CAN WE THWART THEE, M'LADY?

:SNIFF:- A HERO MUST USE THIS CEREMONIAL PUMPKIN CARVER AND CUT A HOLE IN MY HEAD.

JUST CUT A SMALL PIECE AROUND THE STEM SO YOU CAN REACH INSIDE.
uh...
...COULDN'T I JUST SHRINK DOWN AND GO IN--?
NO! THE BAD SEED MUST BE BRAVELY CUT FROM MY MELON.
NO DICE.
WE DO NOT HURT PRINCESSES.
SO, YOU WERE LYING ABOUT BEING HEROES?
WHA--?
LADY, WE ARE NOT FIBBERS!
THEN DO IT, FOOLS!
eep.
HEE HEE! IT TICKLES.
SSGLICH!

HEE HEE
giggle
IT TICKLES!
WEEEE!
THIS IS SOME NUTTY JUNK, BRO.
JUST PRETEND YOU'RE A DOCTOR DOING AN EVIL-ECTOMY, DUDE.

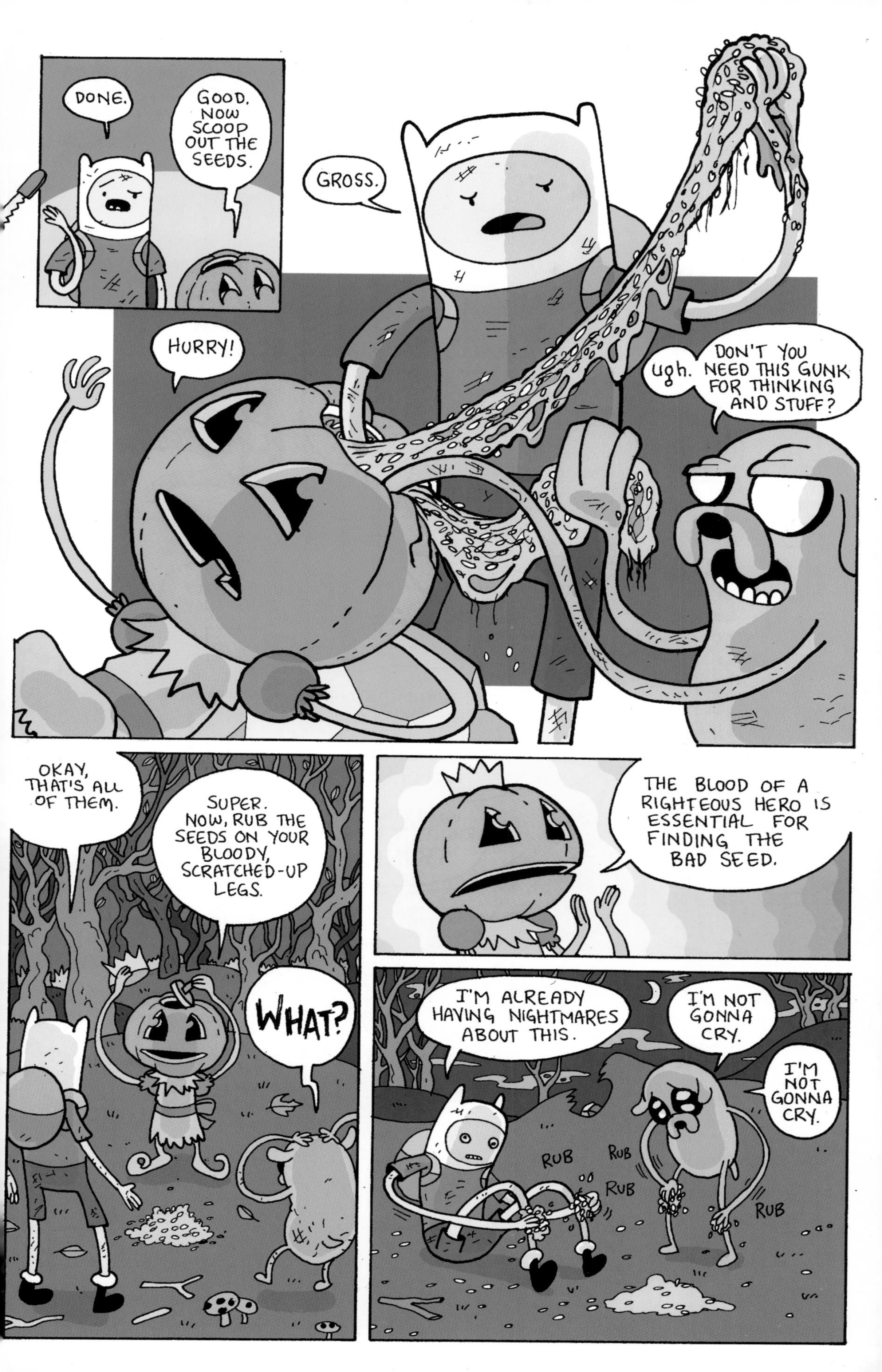
DONE.
GOOD. NOW SCOOP OUT THE SEEDS.
GROSS.
HURRY!
ugh.
DON'T YOU NEED THIS GUNK FOR THINKING AND STUFF?
OKAY, THAT'S ALL OF THEM.
SUPER. NOW, RUB THE SEEDS ON YOUR BLOODY, SCRATCHED-UP LEGS.
WHAT?
THE BLOOD OF A RIGHTEOUS HERO IS ESSENTIAL FOR FINDING THE BAD SEED.
I'M ALREADY HAVING NIGHTMARES ABOUT THIS.
I'M NOT GONNA CRY.
I'M NOT GONNA CRY.
RUB
RUB
RUB
RUB

FINISHED. NOW WHAT DOES THIS BAD SEED LOOK LIKE?
IT'S OBLONG AND PALE YELLOW.
uh... THEY'RE ALL OBLONG AND YELLOW.
YES! MWA HA HA HAAAA
THEY'RE ALL BAD SEEDS.
OH, SNAPITY SNAP-SNAP.
DITTO, DUDE.
YOUR HEROIC BLOOD WAS THE PERFECT FERTILIZER FOR MY GOURD GHOUL ARMY.
ISN'T THAT RIGHT... TREE TRUNKS?
OH, MY YES.
YOU BOYS WERE A BIG HELP.
WHA-?
TREE TRUNKS? YOU'RE EVIL NOW?
OH, NO, NO, NO, FINN.
JUST A LITTLE NAUGHTY.

YOU SEE, PUMPKIN PRINCESS ALWAYS DONATES HER SEEDS TO HELP ME GROW FRESH INGREDIENTS FOR MY SPECIAL HALLOWEEN PUMPKIN PIE.
THIS YEAR WE THOUGHT WE WOULD HAVE A LITTLE FUN WITH IT.
hee hee.
AW, YEAH.
BUMP

WHAT ABOUT ALL THAT JUNK ABOUT NEEDING A HERO'S BLOOD AND STUFF...?
JUST MESSIN' WITH YOU.

BUT THE GOURD GHOUL ARMY...
THEY'RE JUST PUMPKINS.
SEE HOW THEY MOVE WHEN I JIGGLE MY VINES?

YOU **TRICKED** US.
CAN I MAKE IT UP TO YOU WITH A **TREAT?**

HA HA, YEAH, ALL RIGHT.
CRAZY BIZ LIKE THIS **DOES** GIVE ME A SWEET TOOTH.
I GUESS.
BUT I'M GONNA NEED EXTRA WHIPPED CREAM TO PUT THIS ALL BEHIND ME, T.T.
WELL, THEN, WE BETTER HURRY.
FOLLOW ME.
I KNOW A SHORT CUT.

END.

BAD GIRL GONE GOOD

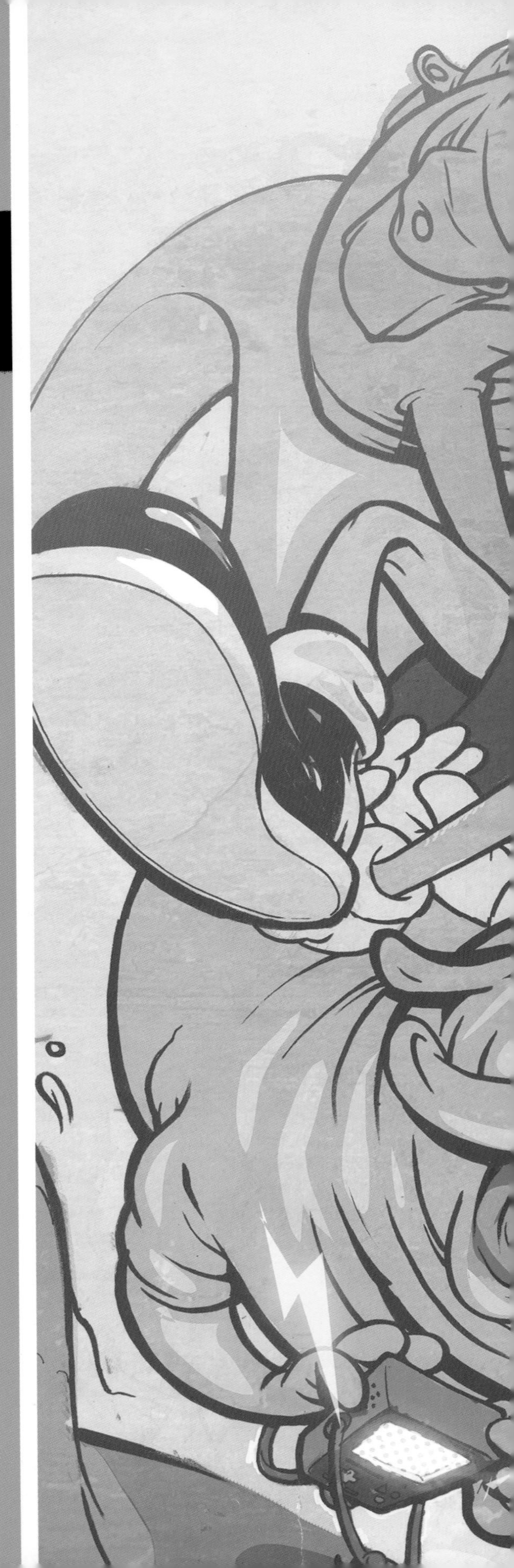

ISSUE NINETEEN, COVER D
CHRIS VISIONS

PERFECT! TOTALLY READY FOR CLUB DIAPASON'S HALLOWEEN NIGHT!
THIS COSTUME AND MY SARCASTIMICE ATTITUDE ARE SURE TO GET ME THAT GOLDEN GAUNTLET AWARD!

BAD GIRL GONE GOOD

WRITER: KEVIN CHURCH ARTIST: JEN VAUGHN

NOW'S A GOOD CHANCE TO PRACTICE.
OH, SCLERA, WHERE'D YOU GO? C'MERE BOY!

Wow! It looks like you've got BIG PROBLEMS there! Anything I can do to help you? Did you lose someone?

YES! MY SCLERA PLUM RAN OFF! I NEED IT SO I CAN SEE!
WELL, I UH... BETTER HELP YOU FIND IT?
er.
Why it's the feastt can do, my friend.
GOLLY! I sure hope I can find it!
HEY! DOWN HERE! I'M SCLERA! HEY! YOO-HOO! HEY!
HEY, I FOUND- I mean, hey! I found Sclera! Hooray!
I'm so glad I got to help you. I hate that I have to leave!
THANK YOU
THANK YOU SO MUCH, YOUNG LADY!
IT'S SO RARE TO MEET PEOPLE AS WONDERFUL AS YOU!

10 MINUTES LATER
SURE, I'LL LET YOU IN!
Even if I'm not on the list? And you don't know who I am? My word that's so NICE of you!
WELL, YOU'RE NICE. NICE PEOPLE GET TREATED NICELY.
USDA
THANKS
REST ROOM
BMO
ON
Thank you! That's so wonderful of you!
YOU'RE WELCOME!
Aaargh
SUGAR
License to Delish
HEY MARCELINE!
HEY, JAKE.
HOW DID YA KNOW IT WAS ME?
SIGH
I CAN SMELL A VAMPIRE FROM 200 YARDS AWAY.
WHAT'S WRONG, SHE-DRAC?

DRESSING UP LIKE THIS SHOULD BE FUN! I SHOULD BE PUNKING THESE PEOPLE!
INSTEAD EVERYONE'S TREATING ME NICE WHEN I'M BEING SARCASTINICE!
I HATE NICE. WHAT IF I'M BECOMING WHAT I HATE?
WAIT A MINUTE, YOU'RE COMPLAINING THAT PEOPLE ARE BEING NICE TO YOU BECAUSE YOU'RE BEING NICE TO THEM---AND YOU'RE WORRIED THAT YOU MIGHT END UP BECOMING NICE AND THAT'S BAD?
GIRL, YOU'VE GOT BATS IN YOUR BELFRY.
(no pun intended)
I DON'T THINK YOU UNDERSTAND.
SCRITCH SCRATCH
GAH, THIS IS GOING TO BE TERRIBLE!
IF IT'S BUGGING YOU SO MUCH, MAYBE YOU JUST TRY BEING YOURSELF FOR A LITTLE BIT?
GO AND DANCE YOURSELF MEAN!

MAYBE MEET SOMEONE WHO'S A BAD ENOUGH DUDE TO KISS---
THAT'S A GREAT IDEA!
UNTZ UNTZ UNTZ UNTZ
Hey wow! I really like your sweet moves! We should totally hang out.

WHAT IS HAPPENING HERE? IS HE BEING NICE-NICE OR SARCASTINICE IF IT'S THE FORMER, THAT'S ANNOYING BUT PRETTY COOL BUT IF IT'S THE LATTER I DON'T KNOW WHERE I STAND!
Ggggnnnaaaaahhh!
NICENESS IS FOR SUCKERS
SUCKERS, I TELL YOU!
REST ROOM
Whoa. She got hotter. Way way hotter.
YEAH, THEY DO THAT.
THEY SURELY DO.
END

OPPOSITE DAY

ISSUE EIGHTEEN, COVER C
CAROLINE BREAULT

HERE I AM ON...
Opposite Day
...WITH NOTHING TO DO!
BY SINA GRACE
WITH S. STEVEN STRUBLE ON COLORS AND LETTERS.
JAKE AND FINN ARE OFF DOING WHATEVER IT IS THEY DO WHEN LEFT TO THEIR OWN DEVICES, AND EVERYONE MADE THEIR OPPOSITE DAY PLANS WITHOUT THINKING TO INCLUDE ME!
MAYBE I SHOULD BE THE OPPOSITE OF GOOD AND INFLICT TERROR AND PAIN UPON THOSE UNDER MY REIGN?
OR -- IF IT'S OPPOSITE DAY -- I SHOULD BE THE OPPOSITE OF EXISTING, AND BECOME NON-EXISTENT.
BUT HOW DOES ONE GO ABOUT MAKING MATTER ANTI-MATTER--
NO ONE'S HERE TO PROTECT YOU, PRINCESS BUBBLEGUM!
BE MY BRIDE!!!
... 'KAY.

REALLY!??
REALLY.
REALLY REALLY!?
YEAH, SURE.
AND YOU'LL LOVE ME FOREVER!?
GROSS.
WHAT?
I MEAN... YES.
C'MON TOOTS!
THERE'S TONS TO DO FOR OUR BIG WEDDING DAY!
YIPPIE!
ATER THAT DAY...
NO.
NO.
YES.
NO.
YES.
NO.

A LOT LATER THAT DAY...
SO MUCH SO IT'S ACTUALLY NIGHT...
DO YOU, ICE KING, TAKE PRINCESS BUBBLEGUM TO BE YOUR LAWFULLY WEDDED WIFE?
YES.
YES.
YES!
DO YOU, PRINCESS BUBBLEGUM, TAKE ICE KING TO BE YOUR LAWFULLY WEDDED HUSBAND?
YEAH.
THEN BY THE POWER VESTED IN ME...
BY THE LAND OF OOO...
I NOW PRONOUNCE YOU MAN AND--

DONG

UGH.
AS IF.
THANKS FOR THE MEMORIES, BUT I'M OUT.

FINN?
JAKE?
TAKE OUT THE TRASH.
END.

NINJA PRINCESS

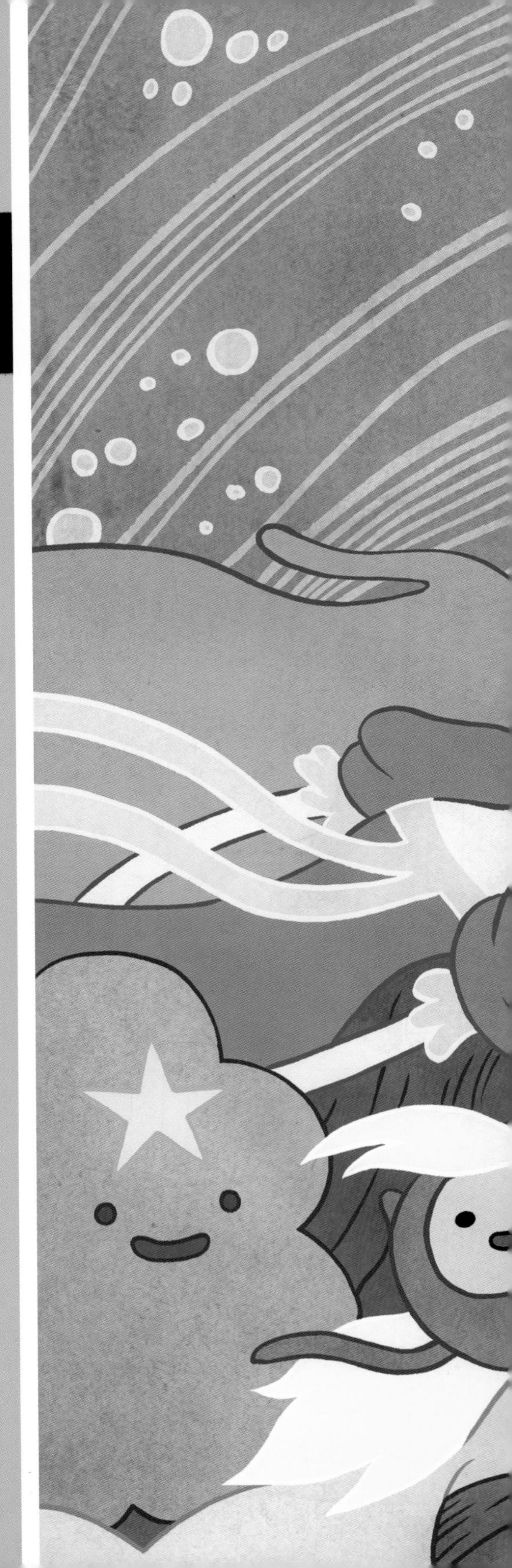

ISSUE SIXTEEN COVER C

SOPHIE GOLDSTEIN

NINJA PRINCESS
Written by Reed, Grant, and Jai Nitz
Illustrated by Pranas T. Naujokaitis

FINN, DID YOU WAKE UP SURROUNDED BY NINJAS TOO?

YES, JAKE. YES I DID.
LOGARITHMIC.

NINJA ISLAND

OH MIGHTY WARRIORS, NINJA PRINCESS HAS BEEN KIDNAPPED BY ICE KING!

YOU ALONE HAVE DEFIED HIS NINJA SKILLS. IN OUR HOUR OF NEED WE GIVE YOU...
THE DREADED FIRE NINJA MANUAL!
FIRE NINJA MANUAL

WHOA!
FIRE NINJA MANUAL

WE WILL LEARN FROM YOUR SACRED TEXT AND EMBRACE THE PATH OF FIRE NINJA SKILLS!
AND BE TOTALLY AWESOME WITH PEWPEW AND FWOOSH!
AND WE'LL SAVE NINJA PRINCESS TOO.

HEY BUBBLE BUTT! WE'RE HERE FOR NINJA PRINCESS!
YEAH, AND WE'VE SKIMMED THE FORBIDDEN FIRE NINJA MANUAL!

YOU MEAN THIS MANUAL?
PROPERTY OF ICE KING

BIFF

BAM

BOOM

DOOM

JAKE! IT'S NINJA PRINCESS!
GRAB HER!

LET'S GET BACK TO NINJA ISLAND!

NOT SO FAST, JABRONIS!
WHACK
GUNTER? IT WAS YOU? WHAT HAPPENED TO NINJA PRINCESS?

A THOUSAND APOLOGIES, FINN AND JAKE. NINJA PRINCESS ESCAPED ICE KING DAYS AGO, BUT AVOIDED DETECTION HERE ON OUR ISLAND.
SHE IS, AFTER ALL, A ROYAL NINJA.

END!

SILLY STRING THEORY

ISSUE EIGHTEEN, COVER
YEHUDI MERCADO

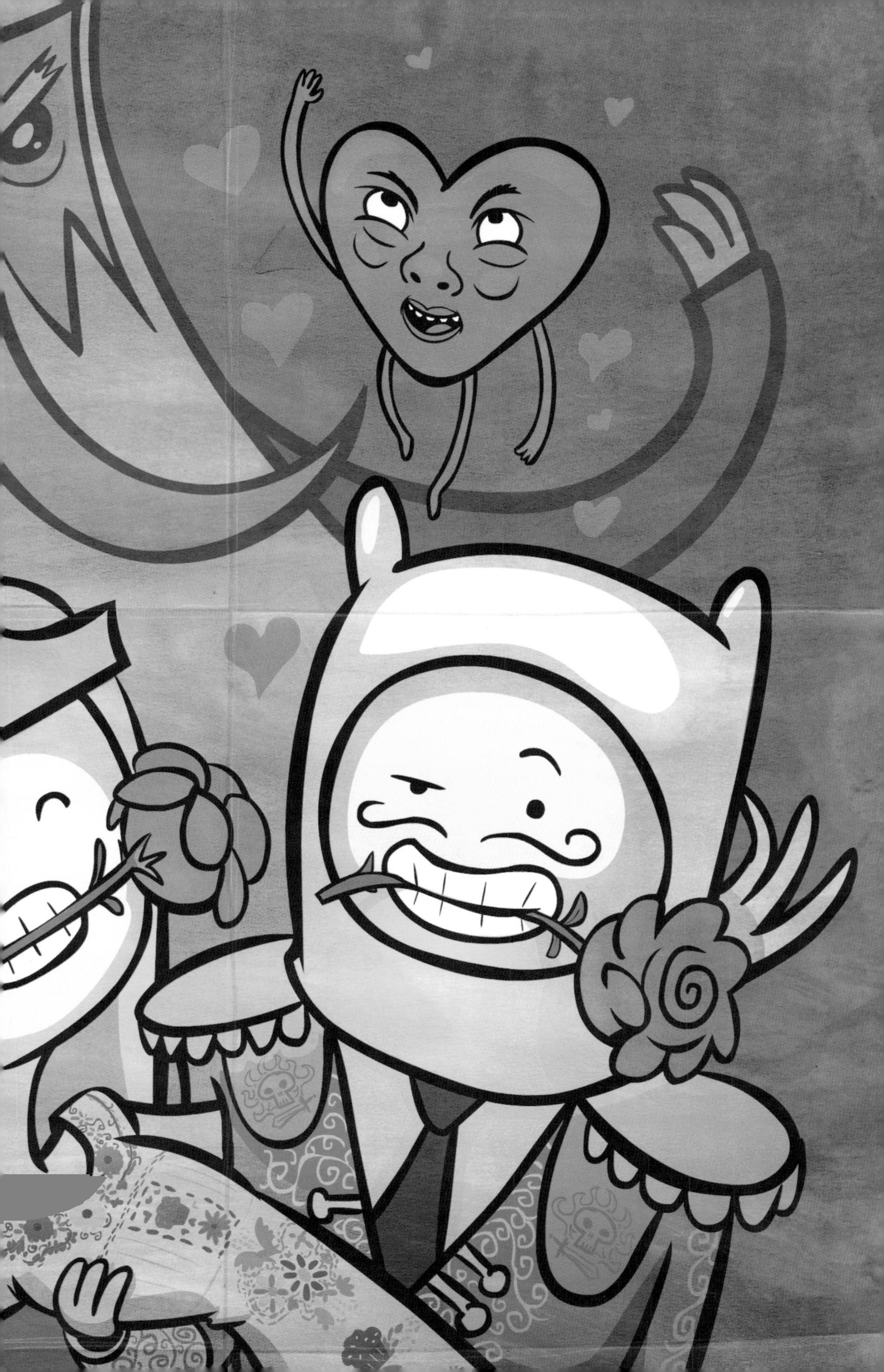

SILLY STRING THEORY
by JAY HOSLER
colors by Braden Lamb
OOO.
I LOVE VISITING YOUR LAB, PEEBS.
THANKS FOR COMING, FINN. I HAVE A BIG FAVOR TO ASK...
OH, SNIKT!
I HOPE IT'S TO TEST DRIVE THIS SWEET, SWEET BABY.
OH, THAT?
NO.
THAT'S JUST MY WEEPING BLADE.
WHY DO YOU CALL IT THAT, PB?
I BET IT'S BECAUSE IT MAKES YOUR ENEMIES BAWL LIKE A BABY THAT WENT BOOM-BOOM IN ITS PANTALOONS.
NO. THE SWORD CRIES ANY TIME YOU FIGHT WITH IT. I HOPE TO USE IT TO END WAR FOREVER.
WHOA. HEAVY STUFF, PB.
IT GETS HEAVIER
BEHOLD THE SILLY STRING THEORY DEVICE.
gasp.
I DON'T KNOW WHAT THIS IS BUT I'M GETTING AN INTENSE FEELING, DUDE.
I HYPOTHESIZE THAT SILLY STRING IS A FUNDAMENTAL COSMOLOGICAL FORCE. AT LEAST IN THE CANDY KINGDOM. THIS EXPERIMENT IS AT A CRITICAL STAGE.
WHAT DO YOU THINK WILL HAPPEN?
?
NOT SURE.
SOMETHING UNEXPECTED I SUPPOSE.

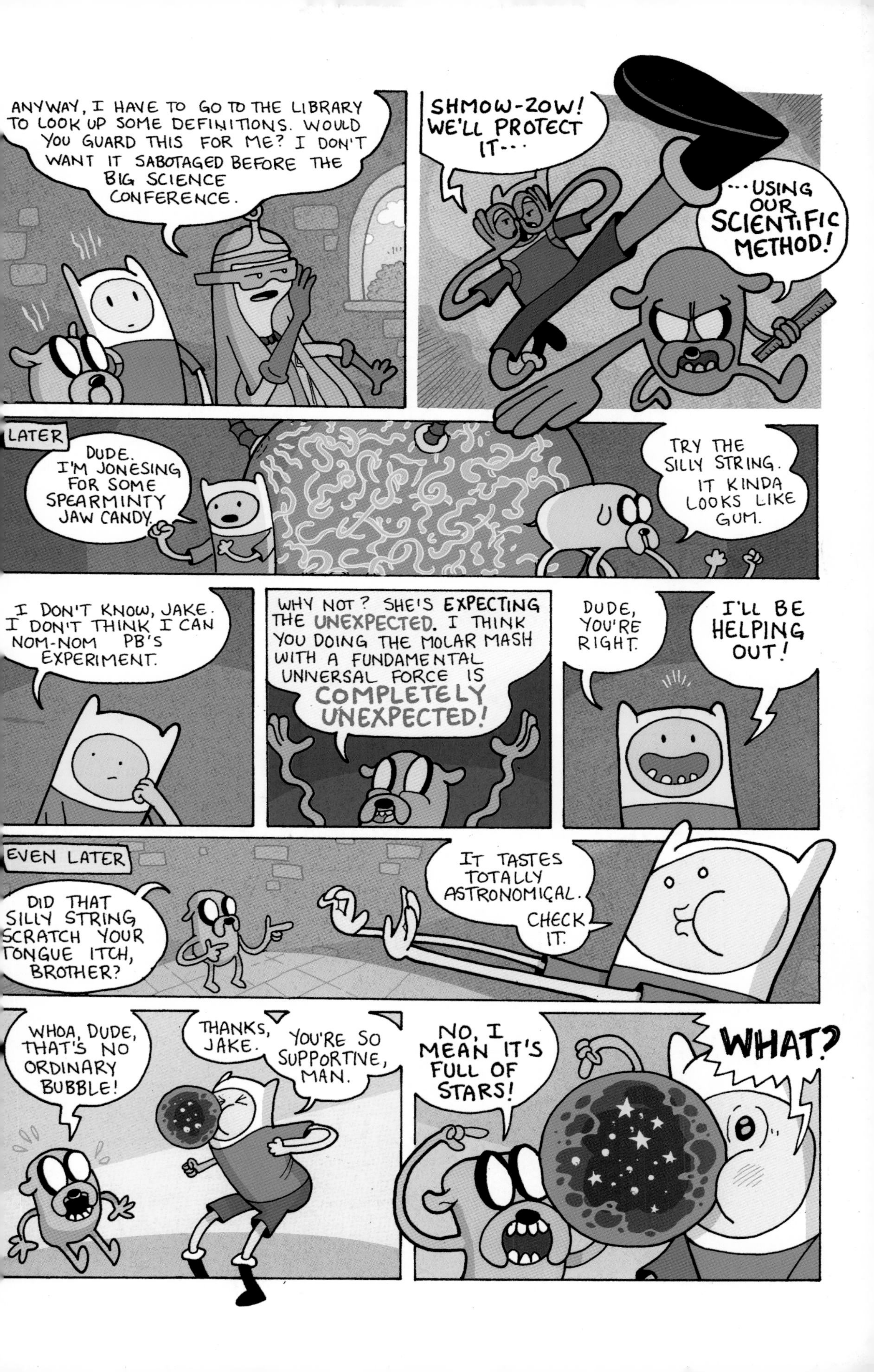
ANYWAY, I HAVE TO GO TO THE LIBRARY TO LOOK UP SOME DEFINITIONS. WOULD YOU GUARD THIS FOR ME? I DON'T WANT IT SABOTAGED BEFORE THE BIG SCIENCE CONFERENCE.
SHMOW-ZOW! WE'LL PROTECT IT...
...USING OUR SCIENTIFIC METHOD!
LATER
DUDE. I'M JONESING FOR SOME SPEARMINTY JAW CANDY.
TRY THE SILLY STRING. IT KINDA LOOKS LIKE GUM.
I DON'T KNOW, JAKE. I DON'T THINK I CAN NOM-NOM PB'S EXPERIMENT.
WHY NOT? SHE'S EXPECTING THE UNEXPECTED. I THINK YOU DOING THE MOLAR MASH WITH A FUNDAMENTAL UNIVERSAL FORCE IS COMPLETELY UNEXPECTED!
DUDE, YOU'RE RIGHT.
I'LL BE HELPING OUT!
EVEN LATER
DID THAT SILLY STRING SCRATCH YOUR TONGUE ITCH, BROTHER?
IT TASTES TOTALLY ASTRONOMICAL.
CHECK IT.
WHOA, DUDE, THAT'S NO ORDINARY BUBBLE!
THANKS, JAKE.
YOU'RE SO SUPPORTIVE, MAN.
NO, I MEAN IT'S FULL OF STARS!
WHAT?

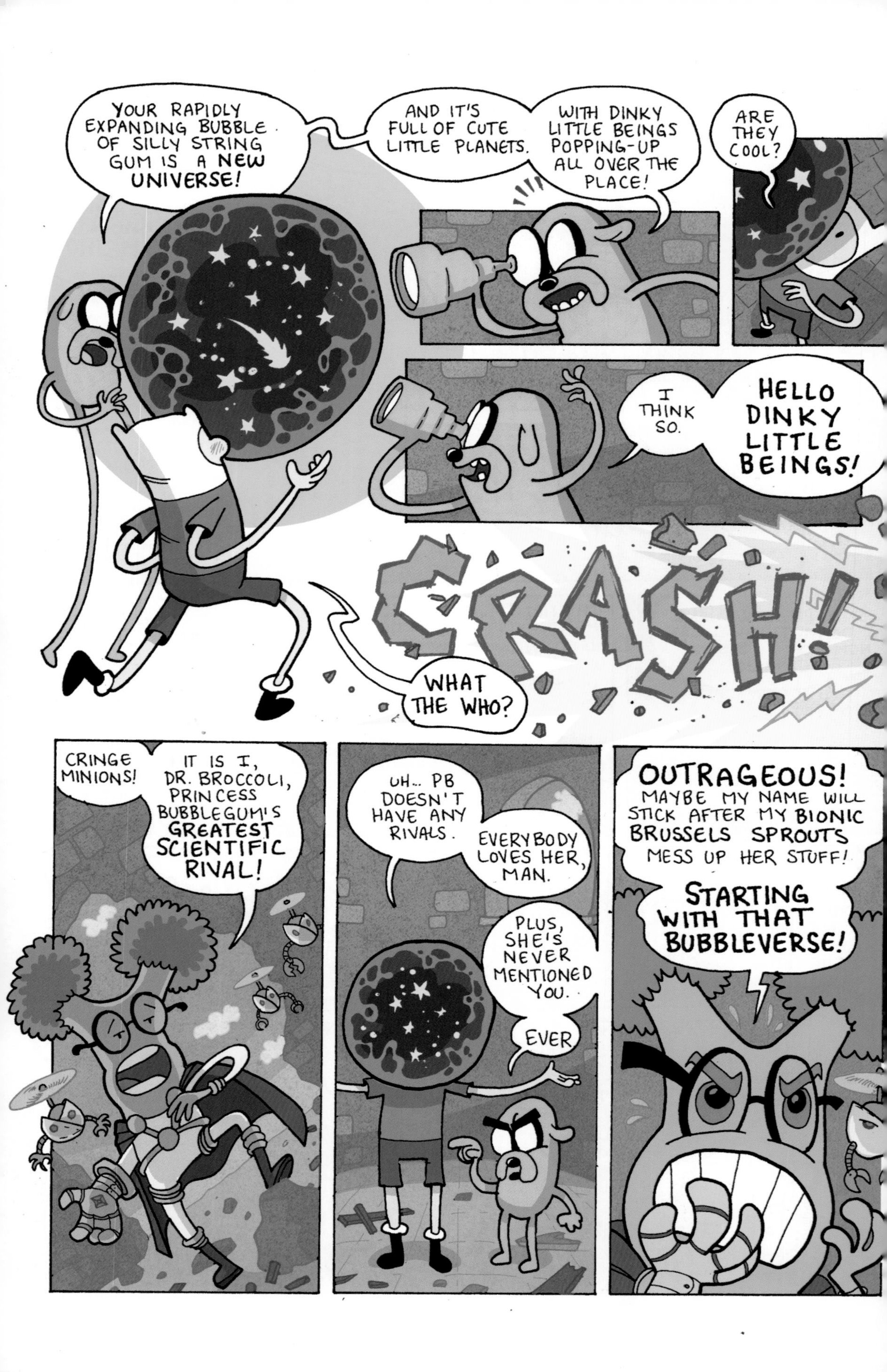
YOUR RAPIDLY EXPANDING BUBBLE OF SILLY STRING GUM IS A NEW UNIVERSE!
AND IT'S FULL OF CUTE LITTLE PLANETS.
WITH DINKY LITTLE BEINGS POPPING-UP ALL OVER THE PLACE!
ARE THEY COOL?
I THINK SO.
HELLO DINKY LITTLE BEINGS!
CRASH!
WHAT THE WHO?
CRINGE MINIONS!
IT IS I, DR. BROCCOLI, PRINCESS BUBBLEGUM'S GREATEST SCIENTIFIC RIVAL!
UH... PB DOESN'T HAVE ANY RIVALS.
EVERYBODY LOVES HER, MAN.
PLUS, SHE'S NEVER MENTIONED YOU.
EVER.
OUTRAGEOUS! MAYBE MY NAME WILL STICK AFTER MY BIONIC BRUSSELS SPROUTS MESS UP HER STUFF!
STARTING WITH THAT BUBBLEVERSE!

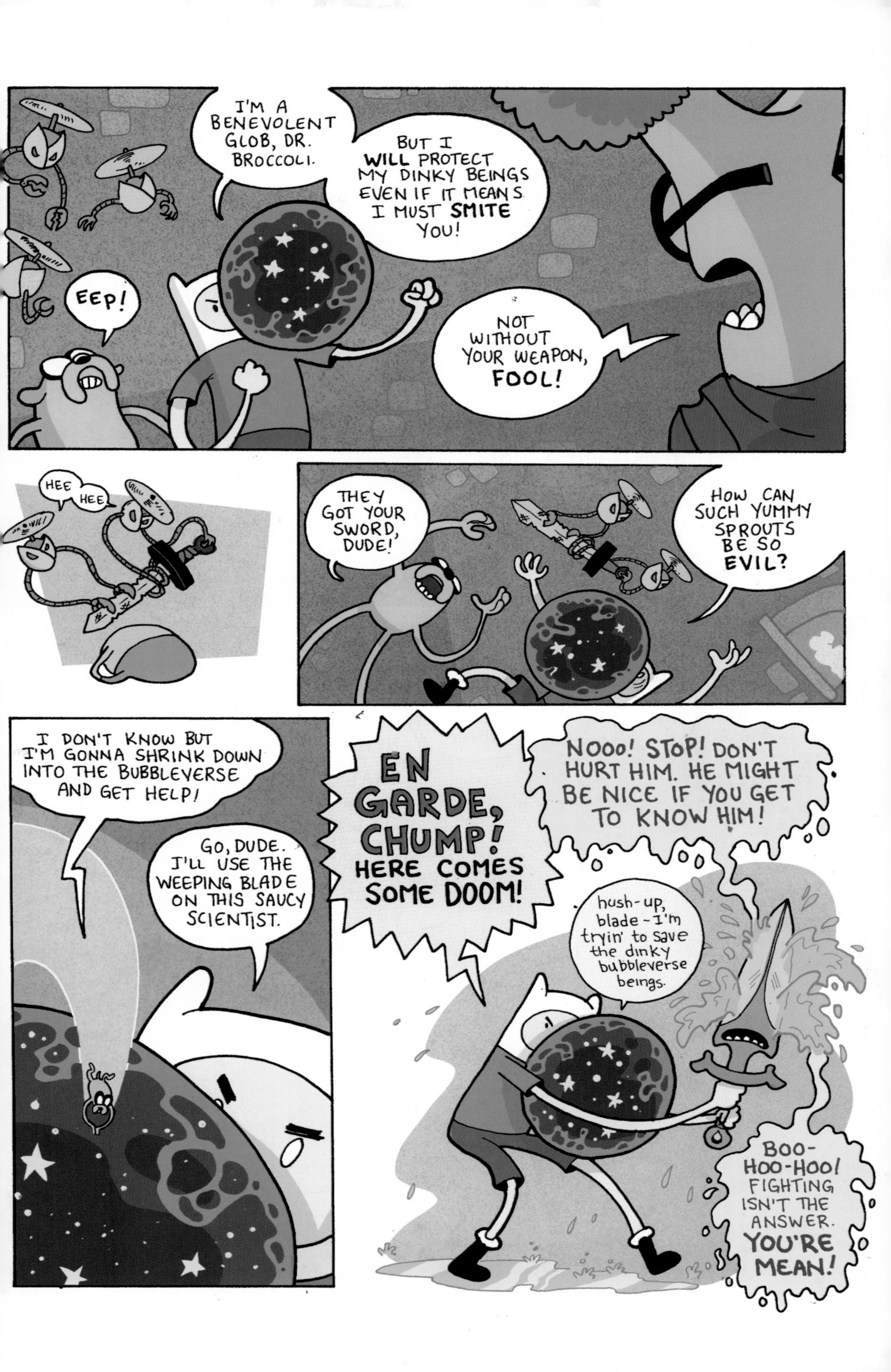
I'M A BENEVOLENT GLOB, DR. BROCCOLI.
BUT I WILL PROTECT MY DINKY BEINGS EVEN IF IT MEANS I MUST SMITE YOU!
EEP!
NOT WITHOUT YOUR WEAPON, FOOL!
HEE HEE
THEY GOT YOUR SWORD, DUDE!
HOW CAN SUCH YUMMY SPROUTS BE SO EVIL?
I DON'T KNOW BUT I'M GONNA SHRINK DOWN INTO THE BUBBLEVERSE AND GET HELP!
GO, DUDE. I'LL USE THE WEEPING BLADE ON THIS SAUCY SCIENTIST.
EN GARDE, CHUMP! HERE COMES SOME DOOM!
NOOO! STOP! DON'T HURT HIM. HE MIGHT BE NICE IF YOU GET TO KNOW HIM!
hush-up, blade - I'm tryin' to save the dinky bubbleverse beings.
BOO-HOO-HOO! FIGHTING ISN'T THE ANSWER. YOU'RE MEAN!

LISTEN TO THE SWORD LITTLE BOY. WHY DON'T YOU JUST GIVE UP AND BAKE SOME COOKIES?
NEVER!
WAAA! WAAA!
GLURG! ... SALT WATER TEARS... SPLASHING INTO ... PAPER CUT I GOT... ..THIS MORNING!
IT STIiiiiiiNGS!
OH, NOOO! THAT'S SO SAD!
HA! HA! YEAH!

WELL, GET READY FOR MORE STINGS BECAUSE YOU'RE ABOUT TO GET THE TONGUE LASHING OF A LIFETIME.
JAKE!
Sniff!

MOMMA? WHY ARE YOU SO TEENY?
NEVER YOU MIND THAT.
YOU STOP PLAYING WITH YOUR FOOD AND EAT THOSE BRUSSELS SPROUTS LIKE A GOOD BOY.
Yes, ma'am.

LATER
BURP!
YOU REMEMBER THIS THE NEXT TIME YOU TRY TO IMPEDE THE MARCH OF SCIENCE.
NOW GO TO YOUR ROOM.

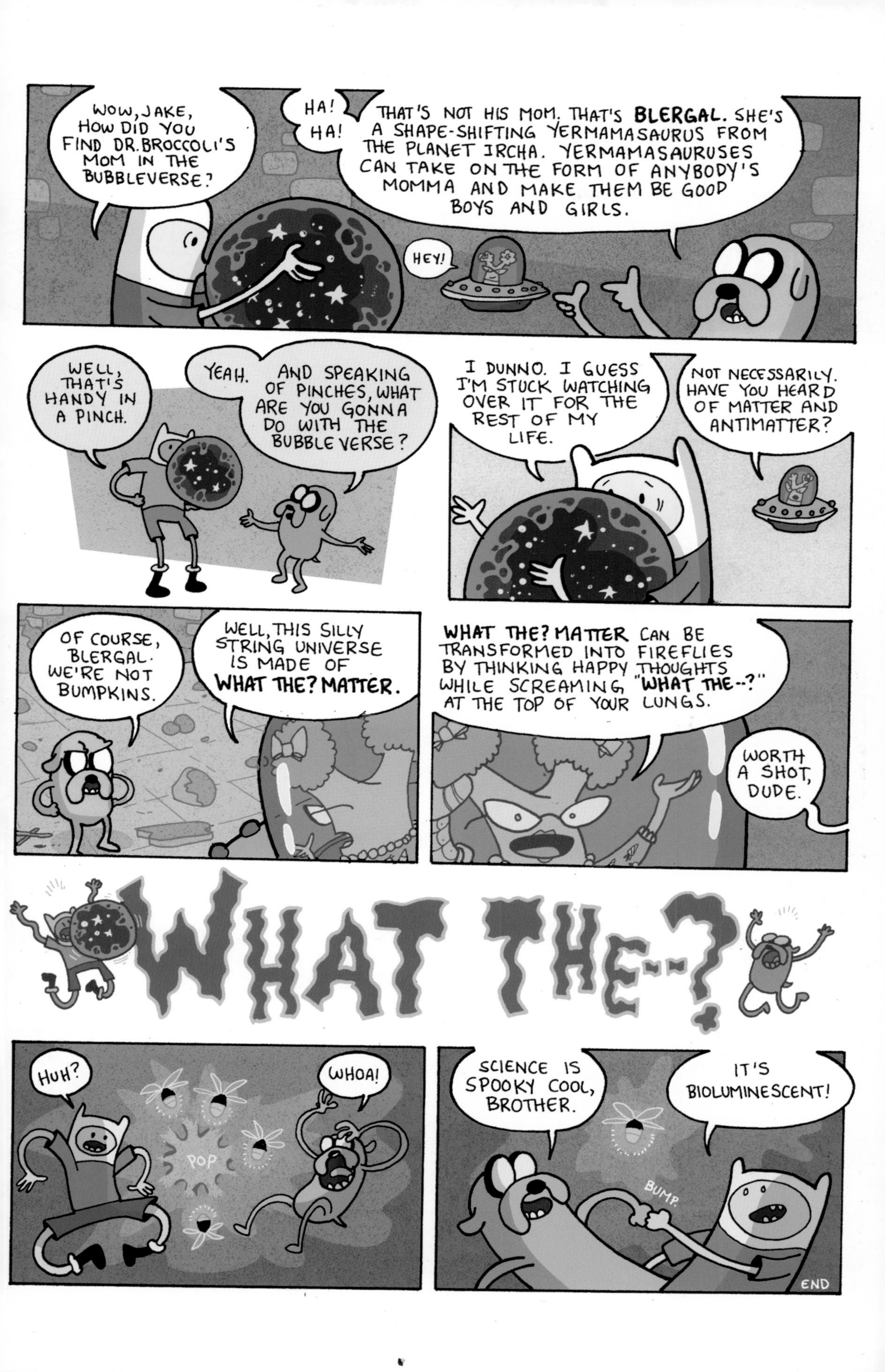

WOW, JAKE, HOW DID YOU FIND DR. BROCCOLI'S MOM IN THE BUBBLEVERSE?
HA! HA!
THAT'S NOT HIS MOM. THAT'S BLERGAL. SHE'S A SHAPE-SHIFTING YERMAMASAURUS FROM THE PLANET IRCHA. YERMAMASAURUSES CAN TAKE ON THE FORM OF ANYBODY'S MOMMA AND MAKE THEM BE GOOD BOYS AND GIRLS.
HEY!
WELL, THAT'S HANDY IN A PINCH.
YEAH. AND SPEAKING OF PINCHES, WHAT ARE YOU GONNA DO WITH THE BUBBLE VERSE?
I DUNNO. I GUESS I'M STUCK WATCHING OVER IT FOR THE REST OF MY LIFE.
NOT NECESSARILY. HAVE YOU HEARD OF MATTER AND ANTIMATTER?
OF COURSE, BLERGAL. WE'RE NOT BUMPKINS.
WELL, THIS SILLY STRING UNIVERSE IS MADE OF WHAT THE? MATTER.
WHAT THE? MATTER CAN BE TRANSFORMED INTO FIREFLIES BY THINKING HAPPY THOUGHTS WHILE SCREAMING "WHAT THE--?" AT THE TOP OF YOUR LUNGS.
WORTH A SHOT, DUDE.
WHAT THE--?
HUH?
POP
WHOA!
SCIENCE IS SPOOKY COOL, BROTHER.
IT'S BIOLUMINESCENT!
BUMP
END

PUBLISH OR PERISH

ISSUE NINETEEN, COVER C

MATT SHEEAN

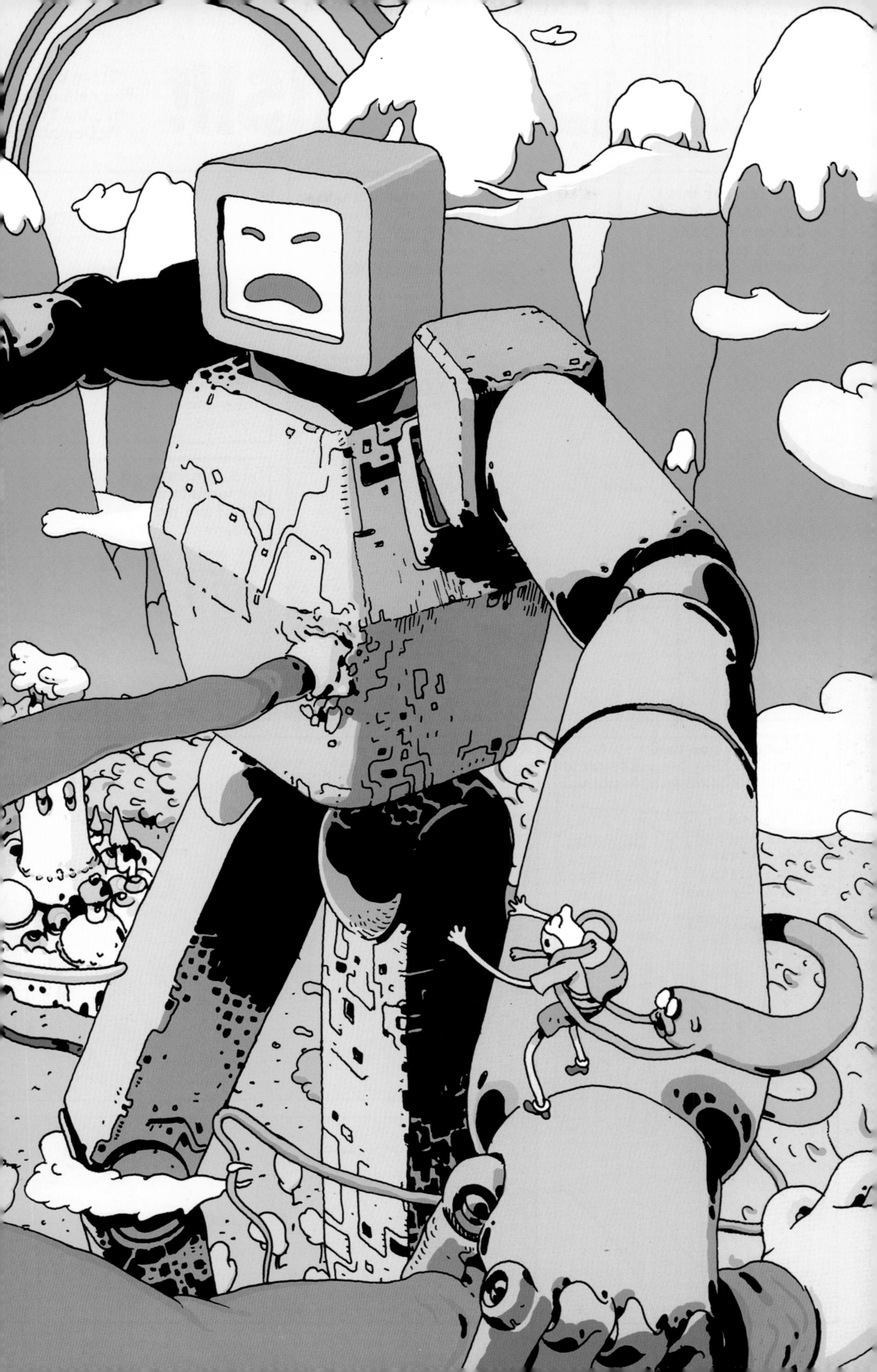

PUBLISH OR PERISH!

Story by Rachel Edidin
Art by Kel McDonald

Why-wolves!
Man, I thought this spy business would be more interesting.
It's worth it! With Princess Bubblegum among our ranks, the Why-Wolves will be... UNSTOPPABLE!
hey must be
nning to turn
r into a Why-Wolf!
Dude, that is a SUPER-DASTARDLY plan! Let's stop 'em here and now.
COUNTER-ESPIONAGE!
We caught these miscreants mid-lurk!
Tell her about the dastardly deeds, bro!
Good work, guys!
hey were
ing to turn
u into a
hy-Wolf!
What?!
WHAT?!
They said once you were among their ranks they'd be...
UNSTOPPABLE!
Hmm. That certainly sounds suspicious.

Is this true?
Yes! No! We never intended to bite you.
Barring unforeseen bloodlust.
Yes, well, except for that. But we have it under control.

Then WHY were you lurking outside my secret lab?
We just wanted to talk to you!
You see, Princess, with your cooperation, we can finally achieve the one thing the Why-Wolves have sought since time immemorial!
Gold?
Political clout?
Immortalit
Sweet jams?
Smoooooches?
TENURE!
As you know, Why-Wolves are slaves to the spirit of inquiry (and bloodlust). We want nothing more than entry to the Ivory Tower to engage in spirited discourse with our intellectual peers, but, alas, we are barred from entry because we lack certain... institutional credentials.
However, co-authorship with a respected natural philosophe such as yourself would be a sure ticket in the door.
So you just want me to collaborate on a paper with you?
What about the bloodlust?!
We will sublimate it into our studies.

uys, I think
ey're on the
level.
All right, but we're gonna stick around, so you'd better not try any funny business.
'Cause we skipped lunch, so we've got plenty of room for SPY-PASTE SANDWICHES.!

Okay! Let's get ACADEMIC!

RESEARCH!

We've done it, guys! Not only
new Unified Field Theory, but ALSO
full accounting of its lexicographical
nplications! That should be MORE
an enough to get you in -- with honors!
Phase one, COMPLETE!
Ivory Tower, here we come!

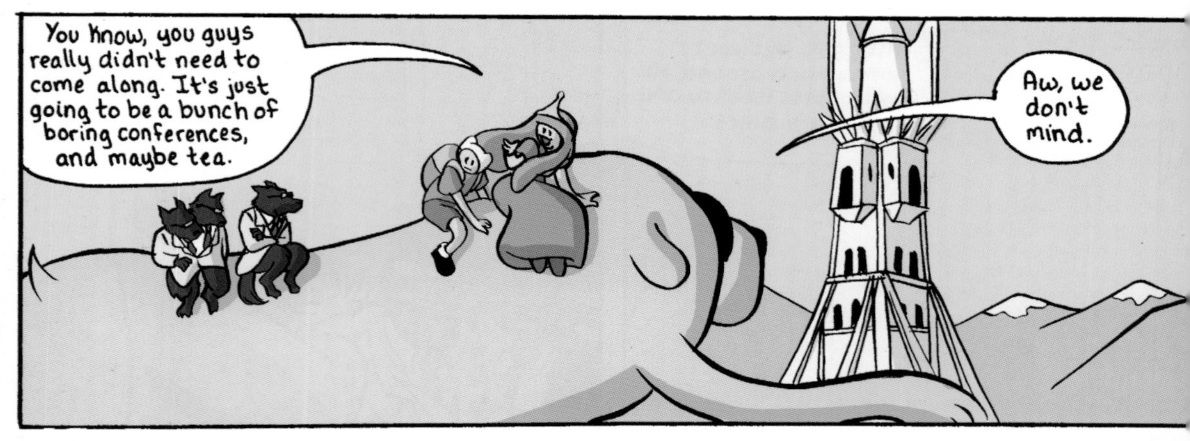
You know, you guys really didn't need to come along. It's just going to be a bunch of boring conferences, and maybe tea.
Aw, we don't mind.

Plus, we didn't want to leave you alone with... you-know-who.
Finn, they've been nothing but perfect gentlemen! And their insights into non-perturbative superstring solutions are absolutely unprecedented!

At last! We stand at the threshold of destiny!
I can almost taste it...
sweet, red destiny...

Scholars only!
No CV, no entrance!
Don't worry, guys. We'll be just inside.
Well, we'll be right here in case of HIJINKS.
So, no funny business!

I wonder what they're up to in there.
Let's find out!

And so, you see, if
ou carry the final four,
verything becomes clear!
Huh, they seem pretty legit. Maybe we really did misjudge them.
Brilliant!
Revolutionary!
And now, it's
me to get down
o business.
Fortunately,
we have formulated a solution to our dilemma. Soon,
we will take our rightful place at the heart of this institution.
For too long, Why-Wolves have been relegated to the extreme fringes of academia.
--ONCE EVERYONE IN IT IS A WHY-WOLF!
TOTALLY called it.
Princess Bubblegum! Over here!

I'm sorry, P.B. I
now you really liked
orking with them.
At least they'll be contained. AND I'll have a stable population of test subjects for my new de-transformifying serum!

Dude, do you think she planned this?
NO WAY! P.B. wouldn't-

Oh, and good work finding a pair with stable phenotypes! Otherwise this would've been a total waste of time.
THE END.

ADVENTURE TIME
TM
SUGARY SHORTS
Volume Three
COMING IN 2017!